Elizabeth

SHENANDOAH BRIDE

SARAH LAMB

A thank you to my proofreader, Brooke, and all of the lovely women who help ARC read to catch those typos I miss!

This book was not written by AI. Any typos are proudly (and embarrassingly!) my own human created ones!

This book is not allowed to be used in training AI.

Paperback ISBN: 978-1-960418-49-4

Large print ISBN: 978-1-960418-50-0

Contents

To all those searching for home, may you soon find it.

Chapter 1

July 3, 1936

President Franklin Roosevelt held a hand up. Once the assembled crowd grew quiet, he began to speak. Like everyone else in the audience, Elizabeth Lawrence tried to pay close attention so she wouldn't miss a word of what he had to say. After all, this was a momentous occasion. A moment that would go into history books, that people would remember for the rest of their lives, and be the start of something incredible.

But none of that changed the fact that she was here, and Robbie was back home. Without her. And that was terribly distracting. What was he doing? Was he missing her? Or, more likely, was he talking with someone else?

Puppy love, her mother had called it, but Elizabeth knew it could be so much more than that. If she could get Robbie to pay more attention to her. That's why she was feeling worried. Two weeks was a long time to be away. What if he forgot about her?

"The president is about to speak," Elizabeth's father said. "Are you paying attention?" His stern expression made her squirm slightly.

"Yes, I am," Elizabeth assured him, bringing her attention back to the present as she let her eyes roam around the crowd.

The buzz of excitement didn't die once the president did start his speech. Newspaper reporters scribbled on pads of paper, and someone with a camera was taking photographs. It was a beautiful day for the opening of Shenandoah National Park. The sky was blue with only a few white clouds, a gentle breeze blew, and the air smelled so fresh.

"We seek to pass on to our children a richer land, a stronger nation," the president said, and Elizabeth's heart swelled at the words as she imagined the future visitors coming here. "I, therefore, dedicate Shenandoah National Park to this and succeeding generations of Americans for the recreation and for the re-creation which we shall find here."

The applause was overwhelming. There were cheers, whistles, and smiles all around. And Elizabeth was right in the middle of it. She could hardly believe it. She was glad she'd come. This was a history-making moment, and she'd been witness to it!

On all sides of her, the excitement and enthusiasm of being here today filled the air. How could anyone not feel thrilled by the president's words? Elizabeth knew she had been.

When her father had told her and her mother that they'd be attending the newest national park opening, Elizabeth had been surprised. Not only had his words been unexpected, but she had wondered what was so magnificent about this place that it warranted two weeks away from their Pennsylvania home? Two whole, long, boring weeks without Robbie?

Though it had been the talk of the newspapers as the first national park in the east, she hadn't imagined they would be there opening day. Why would they? What was so special about it?

Now, as she looked around her, Elizabeth was glad that they were here. Even if Robbie wasn't. Absence makes the heart grow fonder, her mother had said when they were leaving home. It must be true, because right now, she positively ached. And she refused to listen to that tiny voice whispering in her mind that Robbie likely didn't even care.

As she and her parents made their way toward the area of the campground they were to occupy during their stay, pushing past excited couples and children running around, along with a leashed dog here and there, Elizabeth's eyes feasted on the area around them. She wasn't sure she'd ever seen so much unspoiled beauty.

The drive there had been stunning as they drove up the Skyline Drive. The road wasn't fully finished, but once it was and there were more vehicles, she was sure the park would be even busier.

More than once, she'd held her breath as her father slowly drove through the park. At times it was because of the twists and turns and the funny feeling those gave her stomach at the idea of tumbling down the steep drop-offs, and others for the absolute beauty that she couldn't believe she was witnessing.

What would she tell Robbie first when she got back home? She knew she'd tell him about Black Rock Overlook. Her father explained how the Civilian Conservation Corps, which was a government program created during the Great Depression, built the overlooks they'd be visiting. Robbie wasn't really interested in nature, but perhaps he'd still find that interesting?

Elizabeth had felt a little dizzy as she peered out over the panoramic vista. Stunning forests and glimpses of the farmland incredibly far below made her feel so small in comparison.

She hoped she'd remember everything they saw today, both so she could write it in her journal, and so that when she wrote Robbie, she wouldn't miss a detail, the way she was missing him. Would he read her letters? How was the mail service here? She hoped they'd arrive before she did, so he knew she was thinking of him.

She couldn't start her letter while driving. They were seeing too much, and the twists and turns made it impossible to write. Elizabeth wanted to make sure she told him about Dickey Ridge Overlook. There, the mountains swept toward the perfectly blue sky, and the valley below seemed as though it were little more than a speck. A dollhouse garden size, it looked so tiny.

And now that they were inside of this majestic national park for two weeks, she wondered what else they might see. Wildflowers? Animals?

"I want to find one of the waterfalls," Elizabeth's father said, standing with his hands on his hips. "I hear there are several in the park. I wonder which direction we ought to go."

"Should we go now, dear, or should we wait until the guide takes us?" her mother asked. "I wouldn't want to get lost. We must also unpack." She turned to Elizabeth. "You have your sketchbook and pencils?"

"Yes, Mama. Right here in my handbag," Elizabeth said, patting it. "I look forward to sketching out some of the plant life I run across."

"And perhaps write Robbie a letter in the evenings?" her mother teased.

Elizabeth flushed slightly. "The thought had crossed my mind," she said. "After all, this is a historic occasion. He might like to learn what we see."

Her father just grunted, and her mother gave a small laugh. Elizabeth tried not to feel annoyed. She had the feeling neither of her parents really liked Robbie. The son of a lawyer, they'd met in the halls of the University of Pennsylvania when Elizabeth was leaving her father's classroom after dropping off some papers he'd left at home.

It had been attraction at first sight, and for the next few months, Elizabeth and Robbie had enjoyed spending time together. They'd visited outside concerts in the park, had tea and cakes or buttered bread in cafés, and attended lectures at the university. She knew she'd miss him while they were gone. Just...would he miss her?

Robbie was quite handsome, and there were many times Elizabeth had caught his attention wandering toward other women while they were together. But, he was twenty-three, and she was twenty-one. That happened at times while one was still young, didn't it? It didn't mean he wasn't interested in her. Simply that—

"Elizabeth, grab my bag of paints, won't you?" her father huffed as he pulled on her mother's suitcase.

"Yes, Papa," Elizabeth said, moving toward the bag he'd indicated.

"I can't wait to paint these stunning landscapes," her mother murmured, turning slowly in a circle. "I'll hang one in the dining room."

"I wish I had your talent with a brush," Elizabeth said, hoisting the bag's strap onto her shoulder, stumbling a little under the weight.

"You sketch quite well," her mother encouraged her. "Don't think less of yourself for not painting. Perhaps you'll do so much drawing while you are here, you'll fill your new sketchbook."

It was true, she could sketch. But Elizabeth wanted to capture every detail around them. The stunning blues of the mountains in all their lovely shades, the rich green forests, the distant buildings dotting the valley below. All of the scenery was so breathtaking, she didn't want to forget any of it once they'd left.

It seemed, even with colored pencils, that might be hard to do. It wouldn't be quite the same. But nothing was, when captured by the pen or brush. Beauty and art, her parents always reminded her, were subjective. Colors were too, perhaps. The main thing was to get enough of a memory so that she could recall it more vividly when she looked back on their time here.

"There," her father said as they dropped the last of their bags at the large tents they'd call home for the next two weeks. Her father had pitched them, and placed them side by side, so that it made one large building. Inside it was quite cozy. Her parents would sleep on one side, she on the other.

"What now?" her mother asked. "An early dinner?"

"That sounds just fine," her father agreed. "All this fresh air is giving me an appetite." He patted his stomach.

An hour later, Elizabeth and her parents were eating cheese sandwiches and a stew that had been warmed over the campfire. They sat quietly, just enjoying the rustling of the leaves in the evening breeze, the snapping of the twigs in the fire, and the faint sound of laughter from other campsites.

It was a far cry from the constant bustle of the city back home. Philadelphia was lively. There was always something to do or see, but it was also crowded and noisy. Even in the city parks, Elizabeth could hear cars and horns and constant noise. Here, it was so different. Quiet.

"This place is everything and more than they talked about in the news," her mother said, as she drank from the tin mug she was holding.

"I agree, and I have the feeling," Elizabeth's father said, offering Elizabeth the tin of cookies, "something is going to happen here to change all of our lives." He grinned then. "Heard that on the radio about the park as well. Just being here, I sense it."

As her mother nodded in agreement and poured herself more tea, it was all Elizabeth could do not to laugh. What on earth could happen on a peaceful family trip to change all of their lives?

Chapter 2

"Coming through," a man, holding more bags than Kyle Struggs was sure he'd need, bellowed as he pushed past.

"Some of these visitors to the park are a little..." Ranger Jeffs stopped and shook his head with a grimace that Kyle felt over every inch of him.

"I agree." Kyle picked up the duty roster that had slipped from his hands as the man barreled past him and furrowed his brows as he studied it. "Wait, I'm a private guide today? I thought I was leading a group."

Jeffs shrugged. "You were. But the family asked for a private guide. Matter of fact, asked for you by name."

"Wonder why. I don't know them. A private tour? We don't have enough rangers for that," Kyle protested. "Have them join with a smaller party if they don't want a large group."

"Nope. Can't do that."

"And we can't cater to the whims of everyone who comes here. We don't have the manpower to do this for everyone who wants a private guide." Kyle thrust the roster at Jeffs. "Soon as other visitors see me leading a single family, they'll wonder why they don't get special treatment. We can't do it."

"We can when it comes from the top," Jeffs said, pointing upward.

"The superintendent?" Kyle asked doubtfully. At Jeffs's nod, his jaw dropped. "You think this visitor made a private donation?" Kyle asked, his eyes widening slightly. It shouldn't have surprised him, the request to get special treatment. Some folks were like that. He'd just never been asked to lead one of them. Kyle was twenty-four, nearing twenty-five, but growing up in an average family on a partial work scholarship to a larger school, he'd seen firsthand how some people acted.

"Don't know, and not my place to find out," his friend laughed. "But you know the areas to keep them out of. The ones not patrolled enough. Once we get more rangers in here, we can, hopefully, keep out more of the people who don't belong and are up to no good."

With a small headshake and a deep breath to try and calm his frustration, Kyle worked his way out of the cluster of guides and tourists, and headed toward the groups of visitors who were lining up for tours in front of a picnic area. Might as well get this started.

His eyes roamed, looking for a family standing alone. If he didn't find the Lawrence family soon, he'd call for them. He wondered what they'd be like. His eyes swept over the tourists. Groups of excited faces met his gaze. Everyone seemed happy to be here. He didn't blame them. This was a historic moment, and the Shenandoah National Park was nothing if not stunning.

He just couldn't help but wish he was leading a group, and not a family. Kyle didn't like the idea of being a personal guide for a well-to-do family, since that's what they obviously were, with a large donation to ensure his services. That likely meant they'd be bored. Ask preposterous questions. Demand to be shown places that were far too dangerous for them to trek to. Or else, they'd complain the entire time. Maybe even demand he be their errand boy.

Kyle had been warned during his training that might happen, and he'd need to keep a cool head about himself. He just hoped he could. Putting up with entitled visitors wasn't what he'd expected when he became a park ranger. He thought he'd be helping preserve nature. Not babysitting. But Kyle prided himself on a job well done, no matter what it was. This would be no different. Who knew? He might even luck out, and find the group were nature lovers, like he was.

The man who'd pushed past him earlier hurried past him again. "One side, boy," he said as he shoved his way through the tourists.

Taking another deep inhale, Kyle hoped that wasn't Mr. Lawrence. They'd been warned that some of the wealthier families would arrive for the park opening, and many would be fussy, wanting to have "adventures" but in comfort. While they weren't supposed to cater to them, how could he not, if he was a private guide?

"At least it's just for a few more weeks," Kyle said, rubbing absently at his left hip. "When I apply for a teaching assistant position somewhere, I'll be around folks who want to learn. Not be entertained."

It would also be helpful to be in a place where he could rest his leg more, let it heal.

He'd enjoyed his time here over the last eighteen months, helping to get the park's trails and campgrounds ready before it opened, and protecting the lands from those who shouldn't be there. Now that the first visitors had arrived, it felt like all of his hard work was paying off.

Shenandoah National Park had many great changes ahead of it; their plans for expansion were impressive. With as huge as the place was, improvements and new programs would never stop coming. He looked forward to returning one day to see the changes, such as new trails and roads. But he had to heal first. He wanted to be able to hike the forests without constant pain.

The higher-ups had offered a job at the visitor's center, not wanting to lose him, and Kyle almost accepted, but something kept telling him that wasn't the right place for him, so he'd turned them down.

He wasn't quite sure where the place he was meant to be was, but one night about a month ago, on an absolute whim, he'd sent a letter to the University of Pennsylvania, inquiring about jobs after another ranger had talked about how he'd enjoyed going to school there. Kyle hadn't heard back, but that hadn't discouraged him. Sometimes mail service was a little slow. They might not even have any positions.

In his letter, Kyle had expressed a desire to both teach others about the natural world, its past and future, and also learn more about it himself. Since he was a boy, all he'd wanted was to learn, and to surround himself with plants and animals and history and books.

He'd be a teacher, an assistant, anything. He just wanted to be there. *Knowledge is important,* he'd said in the letter he'd sent inquiring about the position, *and I want to both share mine and learn more from others.*

He knew that he ought to have contacted more than one place about a job. After all, it would improve his chances. But something kept telling him to wait. Not to inquire anywhere else. So, he had listened, and hoped his instinct was correct.

Kyle rubbed at his hip again, trying to ease the knotted muscles near his upper thigh, and searched the crowd once more. As the various tourists were leaving with guides throughout the different areas open just now, the crowd was thinning.

A family of three stood a short way behind a group that was just leaving with their guide. They looked slightly anxious as they looked around, as if for where they were to be. Kyle's eyes met those of the young woman, who gave him a small smile.

That must be them.

He tried not to stare, but she was one of the prettiest girls he'd ever seen. Which likely meant she was one of the most spoiled. That was how it usually went, in his experience. It would be just his luck that this was his family, and he'd have her whining the entire time.

Kyle forced a pleasant expression on his face as he strode toward them. He didn't know why he was dreading this so much. It might not turn out as bad as he thought. In fact, perhaps a small group would be easier. He wouldn't lose anyone, at any rate, and their questions were likely to be of the simple kind, all things he could answer easily.

Regardless, this was his job and there wasn't a thing he could do about it. Kyle nodded as he approached. "Lawrence family?"

The young woman's curious eyes locked on to him, and it felt as though a jolt of electricity ran from his ears to his toes. A rushing sound filled Kyle's ears, and he felt as though he couldn't catch his breath. Without meaning to, he stepped backward.

What had just happened?

Chapter 3

"Ah! Our first full day ahead of us! While we wait for our guide, we might as well listen to this one," Elizabeth's father suggested, leading them toward another group.

"Yes, it's better than just standing around," her mother agreed, moving a little closer to the crowd.

Elizabeth listened as a guide explained to the large cluster before them, "Within these Blue Ridge Mountains, people have lived for at least 9,000 years."

"My word," her mother whispered. "Imagine that. I had no idea. There is so much history in this place. I pray I can capture some of its beauty and do it justice."

Elizabeth nodded in agreement, not having realized how many people had walked on the same land she stood on.

The guide pointed to his left, raising his voice so everyone could hear. "American Indians who lived in this area hunted game and gathered fruit, nuts, and berries on the upland slopes." He pointed in another direction. "At the lowest elevations in the Piedmont and Shenandoah Valley, and just outside the park, some of them constructed permanent villages."

"Fascinating," Elizabeth's father said as he rubbed his hands together. "You can't tell me too much about other cultures! It's one of my favorite things to touch on when I teach. I cannot wait for our guide to arrive. I wonder what things he will tell us."

"The woods are filled with animal and plant life," the guide said, "and you will likely see animal tracks, and perhaps even spot smaller creatures such as squirrels and rabbits and all manner of flying species, but potentially deer, bears, and other predators.

"There are also snakes, both poisonous and not, but none of these creatures I mentioned or any of the others should bother you if you don't bother them. Please stay together, for your safety. However, some advice. If you do run across an animal who wants to attack, don't worry. You don't have to outrun him, you only have to outrun the slowest in the group. Now, be warned. I was captain of my school track team, so I stand a good chance of outrunning all of you."

There was a moment of shocked silence, then sudden laughter at the joke, as the group started to shuffle toward one of the paths.

Just then, Elizabeth's eyes locked onto a man in a park ranger uniform. He was of medium height, likely not much taller than her, with dark hair and eyes, and though his expression was serious, she had the feeling that when he smiled, it would, as they say, light up a room.

"Lawrence family?"

Her parents' eager faces turned toward him. "Yes, Jim Lawrence," her father said, offering his hand. "This is my wife, Rebecca, and our daughter, Elizabeth."

"It's a pleasure. Kyle Struggs. I'm to be your guide while you are here," he said, giving each of them a quick handshake.

Elizabeth all but dropped his hand. When he had touched her, it felt as though her flesh were about to be seared. It was the strangest thing. Where had such heat come from?

"Is there anything in particular you are wanting to see while you are here?" Kyle asked.

"We'll know just what it is when we see it," her mother said eagerly. "You see, we both paint, and we are looking for the best spots to capture on canvas."

"I see," Kyle said. He grew a thoughtful expression, and said, "I think I know our first stop. Follow me."

Elizabeth and her parents followed behind him toward a narrow trail on the left. They went up a small slope, and were surrounded by trees on each side.

"Feel free to ask me any questions you may have," Kyle said. "I might not know everything, but I do know a lot about the park."

"I overheard another guide talking about how the name Shenandoah came to be," Elizabeth's father said. "But I missed most of it. Do you know that story?"

"I do," Kyle said, slowing down as he pointed to a small stream that had opened before them. "The legend is one from the Indian tribes who lived here. It says, after the Great Spirit made the world, all of the stars came together on the shores of a silver lake that was bordered with blue mountains. This was the most beautiful place the stars above could see.

"The stars made a promise to gather there in that exact spot every one thousand years. One of those times, the mountain wall ripped, and an opening was created. Waters from the lake poured out and rushed to the sea.

"Time passed, and the stars looked all over the earth for another meeting place, but none was to their satisfaction. Eventually, they found a valley with a river that wound through it. Then, the stars realized that this valley had been the bed of the beautiful lake they had loved, and the blue mountains around it were the same ones they had seen before.

"The stars were so happy to have found their beautiful spot again, that they placed the brightest jewels from their crowns in the river where they still, to this day, sparkle.

Since that moment, the river and its valley have been called Shenandoah, Daughter of the Stars."

"What a beautiful story," Elizabeth said, her eyes wide. "I'm so glad we got to hear the entire tale."

"It was fated," Elizabeth's mother added. "Like that pull some people feel toward each other, when they know they are the one." She smiled then at Elizabeth's father, who put his arm around her.

"There is one more piece to your question, Mr. Lawrence," Kyle said. "Some also say that the name Shenandoah comes from Chief Skenandoah. He was born into the Susquehannock tribe, but adopted into the Oneida tribe. He was also a friend of George Washington."

"I've heard of him!" her father said excitedly. "Didn't he help prevent massacres during the Revolutionary War by alerting colonists of approaching enemies?"

"That's right," Kyle said. "And then both Washington and Skenandoah signed the 1794 Treaty of Canandaigua."

"And that's another fascinating point in history," her father said, fixing the guide with a wide smile. "You, son, are a learned man, I see."

Elizabeth fought a smile as the guide's face reddened. "I...I enjoy history," he admitted, "as well as natural science. I'm actually hoping to one day have a job at a university."

"Is that so?" her father replied. He glanced over at her mother with a wink, and then asked, "What do you think? Here? Or keep going?"

"I'd like to go a little further up," her mother said, adjusting the strap of her bag that contained her art supplies. "I do want to paint this stream to help me remember that lovely story, but from another angle."

"As do I," her father agreed.

"Then let's continue," Kyle said.

Elizabeth followed her parents and Kyle, who had easily struck up a conversation with them. It was a surprise to her how quickly they'd gotten along. Or maybe not. Though she'd not spoken much herself, there was something about Kyle that drew her in. Made her want to listen to him talk.

He was attractive too, not that she'd be interested in a man like him. Her eye was firmly set on Robbie. Who...who hadn't seemed disappointed that she was going to be gone for two weeks. That's why she hoped by writing him, he'd miss her. At least a little. Elizabeth bit her lip and tried not to let on she was distressed over the thought as she followed closely up a steep incline. She was a few steps behind the others when her boot caught on a loose rock and Elizabeth slid backward.

"Let me help you," Kyle offered, jogging toward her and holding out his hand.

Elizabeth accepted it, and was surprised at both the strength as he helped her up, and the gentleness in his touch. That heat was there in his hand again, but instead of nearly burning her, it felt warm. Comfortable. Familiar?

"Thank you," she said, once the path had leveled out slightly.

For some reason, that made her remember how a few months prior, she'd hurt her ankle, and Robbie had tapped his foot impatiently as she slowly walked up a set of stairs. Had it been Kyle, Elizabeth wondered if he'd have done more. Offered his arm. Maybe even carried her?

And just as quickly, she wiped the thought away. She had no business fantasizing about a park ranger! Not when Robbie was waiting. Besides, she hardly knew this ranger!

Kyle paused, then asked, "What about here?"

Her mother's gasp was all the affirmative that they needed. A wooded hollow was before them, with a small stream running down the middle. Soft mosses and ferns in several shades lined a few fallen logs. When Elizabeth brushed her fingertips against them, they were as soft and feathery as she'd imagined.

"This will do nicely," her father agreed, already opening his bag. "But there's no need for you young people to sit around. Why don't you continue on? Our Elizabeth enjoys botany. Perhaps you can take her to explore a bit. Point out some plants that are unique to this forest."

"Ah, if you are sure?" Kyle asked, glancing at her.

"Yes, yes, go on," her mother said, not even looking as she set out her canvas.

Elizabeth gave a small shrug. "That sounds fine."

"Then let's go," Kyle said. "We'll go about an hour, hour and a half up, then turn around."

"That's just fine," her father said, unpacking his paints and brushes.

Elizabeth headed along the path they'd come from and heard the park ranger's quick steps as he caught up.

"Anything you'd like to see, Miss Lawrence?" he asked.

"Elizabeth, please," she told him. "And no. I will just enjoy whatever it is you show me."

He nodded, and led her down a small path that hadn't been traveled much. Elizabeth took in the beauty around her. Fungus on trees and mossy rocks, roots that curved up, and the papery, peeling bark on a birch tree.

Neither of them had spoken since they turned on the path, but instead of it being an awkward feeling, it was quite comfortable. Elizabeth found herself relaxing. She glanced at the guide a few times. Dark hair, dark eyes, a slight limp. She wondered how he'd gotten that.

She didn't miss how he'd rubbed at his hip a time or two. They could slow down, even stop if he wanted, she'd be fine with that. But she didn't want to ask or offend him or insinuate he wasn't capable of going on, so she stared into the trees, and lost herself in her thoughts.

"Let's turn here," Kyle said. "I want to show you something."

He offered his hand again. "It's steep for a few moments, but I think you'll enjoy the view."

Curious, she reached for him. He helped her up the steep path. Elizabeth used her free hand to grab onto trees and help push herself upward. She had no doubt if he released her she'd tumble down. Almost as if he'd felt her fear, he looked back at her with a grin. "Almost there. Don't worry. And, I won't let you fall."

She nodded, too breathless from the exertion of climbing to answer. A moment later, she gasped. They were standing on top of a large rock, deeply planted in the rich earth, with twisted tree roots all around. Below them was a waterfall. Even from this distance, she could hear the water rushing.

"It's beautiful," Elizabeth whispered. She realized she was still holding his hand, but didn't want to let go, in part because she was fearful of falling down the drop-off, and in part because...she liked it.

What was happening? She belonged to Robbie. Well, not really. Not yet. They weren't more than friends, but she'd hoped for so much more for the last year. So, why was it that right now, next to the man she'd known for less than two hours, she felt more comfortable and more content than she ever had around Robbie?

Chapter 4

Kyle couldn't stop the smile that appeared at Elizabeth's gasp. He watched as her eyes scanned the waterfall below and just to the side of them, drinking in the beauty.

From this distance, they could still hear the water rushing. If they were closer, it would be much louder. It sparkled in the sunlight as drips tumbled and reminded him of the story he'd told, about the stars placing their jewels in the water.

"This is...spectacular," Elizabeth whispered.

"I'm glad you like it," Kyle told her. "The path is steep to get here, as you saw, and we've not made a proper trail yet, so there are not many people who have seen it."

"I'm glad that I'm one of them," Elizabeth said. Then she added, "And thank you for holding my hand. At this height, my stomach gets a dizzy feeling. I am just a little afraid I'll lose my footing."

At her words, Kyle looked down to see that he *was* holding her hand. He'd completely forgotten. Her fingers, safely wrapped in his, fit perfectly. He hadn't noticed at all, perhaps because it felt so natural? Kyle wasn't sure he'd ever offered his hand before to someone, but with Elizabeth...

He swallowed hard. "I promise nothing will harm you while I'm around."

She turned slightly, just enough to meet his eyes and teased lightly, "Be careful. I might hold you to that."

"You can," he assured her earnestly. "It's a promise I gladly and easily make."

Her cheeks colored just the slightest and she looked away. Kyle was surprised as he felt her shiver, the faint vibration going through his hand. Had he been too bold? He hadn't meant to be.

"Thank you, I appreciate you being willing to continue the tour," Elizabeth said. "What little I have seen so far just astounds me. It's so clean here; the air seems so fresh. If I close my eyes, I think I can hear at least a dozen types of birds singing."

"You likely can," he agreed. "We have so many here."

Elizabeth slowly moved toward him, still holding his hand. "Where next?" she asked.

"Let's go a little more along this path, then we will return to your parents," he told her.

She nodded, and as the path leveled out, they released hands. Kyle felt the loss, and wondered why. He tried to fight the urge to ask the young woman questions, to learn more about her. It would make it all the more difficult to say goodbye later.

Kyle felt badly for jumping to conclusions before he'd met the family. So far, they'd been nothing but normal, down to earth and, in the case of Elizabeth, intriguing.

A time or two she stopped, pulled out a small notebook, and sketched a drawing. "You are skilled," he said, admiring the drawing of the spruce she'd just done. "You draw both well and quickly."

"Thank you," she said, a hint of surprise in her voice. "I appreciate you not minding. It bothers Robbie when I stop for a moment to draw, but it's something I've always done. I want to learn more about the things I see, and I also want to remember them. Sketching these plants will help me do both."

"Who is Robbie?" Kyle asked, before he could stop himself.

"He's a friend, back home. Sort of." She frowned a little. "I don't really know where we stand."

Kyle nodded, and even though he knew he wasn't supposed to ask her such a personal question, he did. "Where is home?"

"Pennsylvania," she told him. "Philadelphia."

"Is that so? I applied for a position at the university there," he told her.

"Really? Papa works at the university. If you'd like, we can ask if he can follow up on your application," Elizabeth offered.

"Oh! No, no, I can't presume," Kyle said, nearly stammering. "But, how interesting. A small world, as they say."

"It is," she said, and then kneeled down next to a small yellow wildflower. "What is this?"

Kyle looked at it, and said, "That's a yellow lady's slipper. It's a type of orchid. There are pink ones as well, but they are quite rare in the park."

"It's lovely," Elizabeth said, sketching quickly. "I wonder if I'll get to spot a pink one while we are here."

"If you watch closely, you might also find some tiny violets. There are still a few left," he told her.

"Then I will watch closely," Elizabeth answered. "I also am curious as to what natural medicines might be here in these woods."

Kyle scratched at his head. "Now that I might not be able to tell you much about. But I can say, there are well over a thousand species of plant life here. So, it makes sense there would be a fair bit that could help a person."

"May I sit?" Elizabeth asked, indicating a large rock.

He nodded. "Go ahead."

She sat down, still sketching, then glanced up. "I don't mind if you want to also rest a moment. There's room for us both."

Sitting did sound good to his hip. Kyle sat gingerly, near the edge of the rock to keep some distance between them. He watched as she almost effortlessly drew a tree stump with mushrooms and moss covering it.

"There's so much here to see," Elizabeth said, bent over her book. "I think it would be wonderful to live here and see it all."

"A few still do," Kyle told her.

She looked at him in surprise. "They do?"

"Sure, since the time the European settlers came, people have lived here. Until the land was bought to make the park, I mean."

"Why would they leave?" Elizabeth asked. "Isn't there room for them and the park?"

"That's a difficult question," Kyle told her slowly. "It's not something I know much about."

"I understand," she said apologetically. "I guess I was just wondering. Speaking out loud. What can you tell me about the people here?"

"Well, the 1750s is when settlers started to arrive here, in the foothills. Of course, they expanded the direction of their land. In the mid-1800s, the land here on the mountain was purchased. Some, for folks to live here and make their homes, others because they saw the beauty and wanted to open resorts for travelers and tourists to enjoy."

"What sorts of houses were built here?" Elizabeth asked, glancing around as if hoping to see one.

"Usually log cabins, many with a single room and a loft. Over time, some people added on to make them bigger. The early roads were made by hand or with the help of mules. Chances are good, you'll even see some of them here and there."

"I can understand why they'd want to live here," Elizabeth said. She pointed. "There's not just food aplenty, but also wood to make tools and homes, things like bark for medicine or dyes. I suppose animal hides could be traded for other goods, and of course, there are berries and roots that can be eaten, and I imagine gardens nearby."

"You seem to know a lot about plants," Kyle said admiringly.

"Is it strange I like them?" she asked, not so much as a question as a thought.

"I admire a person who has something that both interests them, and also is intellectual," Kyle told her.

The air seemed to fill with a heavy feeling. Kyle felt slightly uncomfortable, and tugged on his collar. Elizabeth, however, if she noticed it, only smiled. But it was a sweet smile, and she reached over, just with the briefest of touches on his hand before she pulled back, and said, "Thank you. That is not something most women hear from a man."

He nodded, unsure what to say, and a little worried he might say something that would get himself in trouble or upset her. How was it just a few hours before, he'd been so sure she'd be spoiled? Elizabeth was nothing like what he'd imagined. She was sweet-natured, and intelligent.

"Do you think we will see any of those families?" Elizabeth asked. "I wonder if the visitors here will bother them."

"No, we won't see them. Of the few left, most are old, and have strict rules in order to continue to live here," Kyle said. "I don't know what, but what's what we were told."

"Maybe I'll run across one," Elizabeth said, her eyes lighting up. "I plan to wander around later, sketching and enjoying whatever catches my eye."

He hesitated, then decided he'd better say it. Elizabeth was curious. It was a good trait, but one that could get a person into trouble. Especially in a situation like this. He didn't want to alarm her, but she was so lovely, and so innocent looking, he wanted to protect her. Even if that meant he might end up scaring her.

"Elizabeth," he said. When she looked at him, he continued. "This is very important, and you should be aware. Those few people left aren't the only ones living here. There are also dangerous individuals who find places like these woods to prowl in, and you shouldn't wander alone. Your life may depend on it."

Chapter 5

Elizabeth laughed. Her life at risk? How funny that sounded. But her laughter and the smile on her face faded as she noticed Kyle's expression. Swallowing hard, she clasped her hands in her lap, squeezing them together and trying to calm the sudden racing of her heart. Taking a deep breath, Elizabeth glanced down, made herself count for a moment, then met his serious eyes.

"Who is here that might be a threat?" she asked, nearly in a whisper. Her voice was so soft, she could hardly hear it.

A sparrow fluttered past them, landing on a low-hanging branch and chirping at her. Ordinarily, the sight and closeness of the bird would have made Elizabeth smile in delight, but right now, she was feeling rather anxious. She glanced around, as if someone were lurking.

He sighed, and ran a hand through his dark hair. "I didn't mean to upset you. Just to warn you. Forests like these are common places for criminals to hide. Not just this forest, but any one. Everyone from bootleggers to thieves, and those who have committed crimes that are even more serious, and are looking for a place to stay low. The outdoors, with such dense trees and shrubbery, far from populated areas, and with hidden caves, have small places where one can hide easily."

Elizabeth frowned. She'd never imagined that. In fact, she could have gone her whole life without knowing such a thing. Now, she felt scared. And confused. "Prohibition is over," she said slowly, trying to figure out that part of his warning. "Are there still bootleggers? Is that a concern here?"

"In a sense," he told her. "The terrain here in the Shenandoah Valley provides excellent cover for illicit distilleries. Both those that operated during prohibition and those that still sell moonshine now. It was one of the ways that those who lived here made money before the national park was created. And it's possible that some still do, and wouldn't take kindly to someone disrupting them."

"I see," Elizabeth said. But then she shook her head, and blonde curls brushed against her cheeks. "Why doesn't anyone stop them? Not so much those making moonshine, but I mean the criminals. The ones here hiding from the law. Can't the government or the rangers do something to catch them?"

"We try," he assured her. "But as I'd said, a place like this is filled with spots to hide. Not just the trees and brush, but there are caves and hollows, shelters that can be built that blend in perfectly and you'd never know if you passed them. It can also be dangerous for a single park ranger to go alone or stumble across them."

"I didn't think of that part," Elizabeth admitted. "That could end badly. Have you had any problems as of late?"

"Not for a month or two," Kyle said.

Elizabeth shivered. "What was happening?" she asked.

"Nothing you or the other visitors need to worry about," he told her. "It wasn't anything that would affect you. It was theft of tools. Equipment. Both small and larger items that are worth some money and easy to sneak out. I really don't think a bit of the trouble comes from the people who live or lived here. It's from those using the place to hide."

She watched as he rubbed at his jaw, a thoughtful look on his face. When he sensed her staring at him, he turned and grinned, though it didn't quite seem genuine. "There's no need to worry," he told her. "Just stay in a group. Don't go by yourself."

Elizabeth nodded, but she felt unsettled and was very glad he was nearby. She couldn't say that, though. How would it sound?

Behind them, there was a loud crack, and she let out a small shriek as she turned. There was nothing dangerous, just a branch leaning against a tree where it had snapped. A fat squirrel chattered at her, its paws holding something it nibbled at.

A warm and slightly rough hand rested on top of hers and brought her attention back to him. "You're safe," Kyle promised. His eyes nearly blazed as he looked into hers. "I won't let anything or anyone harm you."

The air felt heavy again at his reminder, and Elizabeth didn't want to move, didn't want to breathe, didn't want to break whatever this feeling was that filled the space between them. If she could stay here, like this, perhaps even closer to Kyle, something told her she'd never regret a moment of it.

Chapter 6

The walk back to Elizabeth's parents had been nearly silent. Not in a bad way, but in a way that Kyle couldn't quite understand. There was something in the air, a thing that made them keep darting glances at the other. He'd never experienced anything like it before, and wasn't sure what to make of it.

"Have a good walk?" Mr. Lawrence asked, looking up from his paints. He wiped a hand across his brow, leaving a streak of blue on his face.

"We saw a waterfall, and the most unusual flower I've ever seen called a lady's slipper," Elizabeth said, taking out her handkerchief and wiping away the paint on her father.

"Thank you, my dear," he said.

"What do you think?" Elizabeth's mother asked, waving them over. "I'm not certain I've gotten the green correct."

Elizabeth studied her mother's painting. Kyle found himself staring as well. "It's a perfect match," he said, even though the question hadn't been directed at him. "You are very talented artists, all of you."

It was quite true. Each of Elizabeth's parents had captured their chosen landscape perfectly. Mrs. Lawrence, in watercolors, and Mr. Lawrence with his acrylic paint. And, of course, Elizabeth herself drew lifelike sketches. It amazed him to see it firsthand.

"A few moments to allow this to dry, or a little more, and we will be ready to return," Mr. Lawrence said. "My stomach wants its dinner."

They waited a half hour or so for the paintings to dry enough to be moved. In that time, Elizabeth sketched some ferns she'd spotted while her parents packed up their supplies, and asked general questions about the park.

Kyle couldn't help but reflect on their trip back how the day had turned out much better than he'd hoped it would originally.

"We will see you again in the mid-morning," Mr. Lawrence said, shaking his hand.

"Yes, sir," Kyle said, and waved as he walked off.

His day was finished with a little paperwork, and checking to be sure none of the other guides nearby needed help. He was tired that night as he tried to sleep in his bed. There were a dozen of them in the large room of their barracks. He could hear the usual soft snores, someone turning the pages of a book, another person's pencil scratching.

Kyle's body was tired, but his hip and leg hurt so much he was having trouble getting comfortable to sleep. He knew he'd likely walked too much today, but that was his job. Still, it wouldn't be but a few weeks and he'd be able to rest, if he got a job at the university.

What were the odds that Elizabeth's father worked at the very university he'd applied to? Kyle hoped he'd hear about the assistant position. Or any position. He'd wanted to work there, with such a strange pull he couldn't have explained it, and now that he knew there was a chance, even if it was slim, to see Elizabeth...

He sucked in a deep breath. He shouldn't think like that. She'd mentioned another man's name. Robbie, he thought it was. But she'd also seemed uncertain. And it sounded like they didn't have any sort of an understanding...

Kyle shifted. Maybe if they met, he could ask her to one of the little places Philadelphia was sure to have, where they could get a slice of pie and a drink...talk for a while. Get to know each other better.

Kyle lay there most of the night, only finally managing to doze off shortly before the sun rose. With bleary eyes, he dressed, straightened out his bottom bunk, and made his way to the nearby ranger's station to make sure his schedule hadn't changed. He'd have been disappointed if it had.

An hour later, he rounded the path to where the Lawrence family was staying. The three were ready, Mr. and Mrs. Lawrence's painting bags already slung over their shoulders, and Elizabeth carrying a large picnic hamper.

"Would you like help?" Kyle asked, even though he wasn't supposed to touch the visitors' personal belongings.

"No, no, we will manage, my boy," Mr. Lawrence said. "Where to today?"

"I assume you want to paint?" Kyle asked.

"Yes. Will you show us another good spot?" Mrs. Lawrence asked cheerfully, adjusting the strap over her shoulder. "I'd like some flowers today."

Kyle nodded and led the way. About twenty minutes later, he stopped at a large meadow. It not only had wildflowers dotting it, but tall wheat-colored grasses that swayed in the gentle breeze.

"This is magnificent," Mrs. Lawrence said. "You are a fine guide."

"Do you wish to sketch here," Kyle asked Elizabeth, "or would you rather walk a little further like we did yesterday?"

"I'd like to spot those wild violets," Elizabeth told him. "Do you think there might still be some growing?"

"There might," he told her. "We can search for them."

"You young ones go ahead," Elizabeth's father said, waving a brush at them. "Come back in a few hours, and we'll all have a picnic lunch."

"Yes, sir," Kyle said.

He stepped back on the trail, and led Elizabeth further along.

"Why don't we stop for a few moments?" Elizabeth asked, pausing at a large rock.

"If you'd like," he agreed, rubbing at his hip as he joined her, being sure as before to leave ample space between them.

"Do you mind if I ask what's happened to your leg?" Elizabeth asked.

He hesitated, and Elizabeth must have sensed his discomfort, because she quickly added, "You don't have to tell me. I'm sorry. It was so rude of me to ask."

"Not at all," Kyle said. "I don't mind telling you. I just...I didn't want to worry you."

She tilted her head. "How so?"

"Remember yesterday I'd talked about people who were stealing things from the park?" At her nod, he continued, "About six months ago, another park ranger and I were chasing after a man who'd been stealing some of the workers' and rangers' supplies. Tools, clothes, food. We don't have many opportunities to replace some of those things, and him stealing uniforms was very worrying. We don't want anyone to pretend they are a park ranger when they aren't," Kyle said.

Elizabeth gasped. "That is terrible! And that's how you got hurt? Chasing after him?"

"We caught the man," Kyle said, "but he had a weapon. Shot my leg. It healed, but…" he let out a shuddering breath, "it hasn't been able to stop hurting, with all the walking I have to do. That's why I applied for another job. I love it here, but my leg needs some time to heal."

"That's terrible," Elizabeth said, her beautiful eyes wide. "I'm so sorry."

"It's nothing you need to apologize for," he told her with a smile. "Just a part of life. Injuries, I mean."

"I see now just how incredibly dangerous people lurking in the woods can be, and why it's unsafe, even for two of you, to chase after someone," Elizabeth said.

"We got the man, at least," Kyle said. "I just hope he was working alone. We never found out. Who knows? He might not have even talked."

"That must have been scary," Elizabeth said, angling her body near his.

"In the moment, I didn't think about anything but getting him," Kyle said, leaving out the part about how they were still worried. The items the man had stolen hadn't been recovered, as far as he knew. Most importantly, were the missing uniforms. It was something each of the rangers kept an eye out for.

But there was no need to worry her or any of the other tourists. Not if there was no credible threat toward them.

A flicker of red caught his eye, and he squinted, the sun's glare making it hard to see. That hadn't been a bird, of that he was sure. Was it another park visitor? Perhaps telling Elizabeth the story had made him a little jumpy. That must have been it.

But, somehow, he couldn't help it. The fierce desire to protect her, and the feeling that he needed to, was almost overwhelming.

Kyle glanced at her. Golden tresses shining in the sun, a sweet face upturned to the sky, and a content look on her face. Something in his stomach clenched as his heart sped up. Her eyes opened then and met his.

Chapter 7

What was happening? Elizabeth tried to calm her racing heart, her struggle to breathe that resulted in her chest feeling tight. Quickly, she replayed the last moments.

When Kyle was telling her about how he'd gotten injured, Elizabeth had felt afraid for him. She knew he was likely telling a lighter version of his story, not wanting to frighten her. But the fact remained that yesterday, when she'd so carelessly asked why the park rangers or the government did not do something about criminals on the park's land, and he'd mentioned it was dangerous, she really hadn't realized how dangerous—even deadly—it could be.

Kyle had been seriously wounded. Could he have even lost his life? She shivered. That might have happened, especially if he had been alone. As it was, he paid a terrible price. An injury that affected him months later. In fact, it was serious enough it was going to take away the job that he enjoyed.

The air grew heavy in their silence. Unspoken words hung between them, something that had never happened to her before. Elizabeth longed to be reckless, to say something like how empty she'd feel without him. But that was foolish. What was wrong with her? She'd known Robbie for months, yet...in just two days, she felt something so much more with Kyle...a near stranger. Was it fate? Was it just a summer interest? She wasn't sure, but something told her this was different. Special.

It almost scared her, though, how strongly she felt. And she knew she needed to hide it, lest he think her some silly girl. Or, worse, kept his distance from her. There was likely some rule about not getting too close to the tourists.

Elizabeth finally met his eyes. "You are incredibly brave," she told him. "You raced after the man without thinking of anything but helping others. And it's cost you dearly, both in the injury and the loss of this job. I cannot imagine many would have done that."

"I don't know about that," Kyle said, "but part of me wonders if it happened because I'm supposed to move on. That there's something good waiting for me somewhere else. Maybe...maybe even Philadelphia."

Elizabeth smiled. "I'm glad we came when we did. Had we visited next month, you'd be gone, and our paths might never have crossed."

"That's true," he said, giving her a broad smile. "I know we hardly know each other, but I like being around you."

"I like it too," Elizabeth said, smiling at him. Truthfully, she more than liked it. Quickly, she added, "I appreciate you also answering my questions and telling me things about the park. Even though that might not be what other tourists hear. I think it's given me a greater appreciation of the area and its history, and also opened my eyes as to the cost."

"Everything has a cost," Kyle said, letting his eyes drift from tree to tree. "I feel like sometimes we never know about it because it isn't always us who pays the price, but another."

"Like the people who lived here," Elizabeth said softly. "I can't imagine being here for generations, and then having to leave. For tourists. A cost I would never have known another paid for me to see this beauty unless you'd told me."

The thought was almost overwhelmingly heartbreaking. Elizabeth found tears forming in her eyes for the people she didn't even know, but imagined torn from their homes.

"You are a kind soul," Kyle told her. He brushed his fingers against her hand, then jerked back once he realized what he was doing.

"You don't think I'm silly?" she asked, curiously.

Her hand burned where he'd touched it, and she wished they'd come across a path again where he offered his hand to her. Maybe they still would. She longed for him to touch her again.

"Not at all," he said, surprised. "There's not enough compassion in the world. People get so wrapped up in their own doings. They forget that others have difficulties too. I think what you are is special."

Her cheeks flushed. Her tongue felt frozen, and Elizabeth wasn't sure how to answer. She didn't think she'd ever been told anything so nice before. Maybe...maybe she could be reckless. Hint a bit. See if he remotely felt the same as she did. After all, hadn't he mentioned that he felt maybe he was supposed to go to Philadelphia? And that he liked being around her? Surely that meant he felt something. Even if it was small.

"Kyle?" Elizabeth asked.

"Yes?" he answered.

But before she could tell him she thought he was special too, he stiffened, and stood quickly. He stepped partially in front of her, his stance protective, and his hands curled into fists.

"What is it?" Elizabeth gasped, fear now flooding her.

Kyle's eyes were fixed on a spot in the woods. He held a finger to his lips and she obeyed, hardly daring to breathe. Elizabeth watched as his eyes scanned the area. After a moment, he relaxed, but only slightly.

"I thought I saw someone watching us," he said.

"Perhaps another visitor to the park?" Elizabeth asked. But even as the words passed her lips, she doubted them.

"I don't—perhaps." He gave her a tight smile. "You may be right. How about we head back toward your parents? I don't want them thinking I've lost you."

His words, though spoken lightly, and with a bit of a teasing in them, held a slight strain, as though he were pretending everything was well, for her sake. Elizabeth stood, though, and smiled. She would play along, so as to help relieve his stress some. Hopefully, there would be other moments alone with him. "Yes! Let's have our picnic."

She set off toward the way they had come from, but didn't miss the fact he walked close to her, and his eyes never stopped scanning their surroundings. She felt tense, concerned. The air held a different kind of tension now.

She wrapped her arms around herself, and Kyle didn't miss the motion.

"I'll protect you," he promised, even as he didn't acknowledge something was amiss. He gave her hand a gentle squeeze before he pulled it away, and continued his constant surveillance.

Elizabeth didn't know what he'd seen, but she knew it was something to worry about.

Chapter 8

Kyle hated that the day was drawing to a close. The Lawrence family had been generous, sharing their lunch with him. Once more, he'd admired their artistic talent. Elizabeth had even turned the conversation to the university her father worked at, and Kyle listened, asking questions about what it was like to work there, what her father did, and he had to stop himself from asking if he knew anything about the assistant position.

That had been hard, truthfully. Almost as hard as keeping his eyes off of Elizabeth. In the sunlight, he could see a hint of red in her hair, and it captivated him, as did her laughter, at her father's jokes.

Kyle didn't fully relax, though he did feel better with Elizabeth with her parents once more. If someone did disturb them, he could hold them off, and give her and her family a chance to get away. While he hoped it wouldn't come to that, Kyle couldn't ignore the prickles on the back of his neck that warned him something wasn't right.

It frustrated him, too, because he'd been enjoying his time with Elizabeth, when they'd been alone. There had been this current in the air...if he hadn't been in uniform, he might have admitted to Elizabeth he was falling for her.

And it was in part because of that he was worried about what he'd seen in the woods. It had been a relief when Elizabeth's parents were ready to return to their campsite. He could get the family to safety. However, the closer they drew, the more park visitors he saw, along with additional rangers, some in small clusters, others discreetly standing at various trail entrances. As if they were looking for someone.

The feeling that something wasn't right grew at the sight. After returning the Lawrence family to their tent, Kyle wasted no time heading to the ranger station. As he pulled the heavy door open, he spotted Jeffs bent over a clipboard, and headed toward him.

Jeffs looked up as he approached, but before Kyle could say anything, Jeffs asked, "Have you heard?"

"Heard what?"

"It's happening again." Jeffs lowered his voice and looked around, even though no one else was nearby. "Thefts. A few of the visitors had items go missing."

"Another visitor?" Kyle asked, though he doubted it.

"Who stole food and blankets?" Jeffs raised a brow, shook his head, and added, "Plus, the people here aren't the sort to go swiping something from another. Especially not food or blankets. It's suspected someone is using the forest to hide from the law."

Kyle frowned, and furrowed his brow. "I thought I saw someone earlier on one of the trails that's closed when I was with the Lawrence family. He looked familiar. But as soon as he saw me looking at him, he ducked down and seemed to vanish.

"I thought it best not to say anything. I didn't want to worry them, and I made sure to stay with them until they returned to camp. However, it bothers me that I couldn't place the man's face. I wonder if that's the person who was lurking about. I know I shouldn't cast suspicion without evidence, but something about him didn't sit right with me."

"Should we go look for him?" Jeffs asked. "We can get a small group. No one is to go alone. It might be too dangerous. You think it was a guest?"

"No." Kyle grimaced. "He wasn't a park visitor. He wouldn't have hidden if he was, even if he'd been on a path he wasn't supposed to be on. You know how they are when they do something they shouldn't. They act like it's not a big deal, that they are entitled to do whatever it was they did."

Jeffs snorted. "You've got that right."

"And, if it was a guest, they wouldn't have been alone. You know how careful we are to make sure everyone stays together or in a set area. Even when I let the Lawrences paint, I'm not so far away with Elizabeth that I can't be close by." Kyle rubbed at the back of his neck, and the prickles that were making their way up into his scalp and down his spine.

"Elizabeth?" Jeffs brows rose, and he grinned. "She's pretty. Lucky you, getting asked to be their guide. But getting to know her? Careful...that's against the rules."

"No, that's...I mean," Kyle sputtered, hoping his face wasn't red. He tried to latch on to something to take the focus away from her. "Wait, you mentioned that before. Do you know why I was asked to be their guide?"

"I don't. But they asked for you specifically before they arrived," Jeffs said. "By name. I saw the letter when we were getting our assignments."

"I wonder why that was," Kyle said. "I've never seen any of them before."

"If it had been after they got here, I'd have thought that *Elizabeth* might have been taken with your good looks." Jeffs winked at him.

"Will you stop? I'm leaving in less than two weeks. I'd like to leave honorably. Not be fired. How would that look on my record?" Kyle growled.

Jeffs laughed and slapped his shoulder. "I'm just teasing. That was the last of it. But in all seriousness," he said, concern filling his face again, "we'd best keep a close eye out on whatever's going on. This isn't good. If someone is sneaking around, who knows what they'll do next. I just hope it's not hurt one of the visitors. We've a few older couples here. Let's not forget the distinguished guests as well. Thank goodness the president just left."

"I agree. Are we increasing our patrols?" Kyle asked. "Is that the duty list I saw you working on?"

"That's already done. This one I'm making is for next week. Yes, orders from up top. We are having extra eyes on the campsites. Still just one guide per group, and we aren't allowed to go quite as far away. At night, however, we are going to have four men at all times watching over the camps, ones who aren't daytime guides. They'll walk around, keep an eye on everything, and rotate every two hours."

Kyle nodded. It was a good idea. More eyes and hands if something was needed, but he hoped there wouldn't be trouble. The park was filled with families right now, all who were there to enjoy themselves and the nature surrounding them. They were meant to be having a good time, not be fearful for their belongings or their lives.

He wondered if he could find out who would be nearest the Lawrence family. Maybe they could keep an extra watchful eye on Elizabeth. He hadn't wanted to frighten her earlier, and he didn't want to mention it to Jeffs, but the man he'd seen in the woods earlier hadn't been looking at him.

He'd been watching Elizabeth.

Chapter 9

"Did you find out anything, Jim?" Elizabeth's mother asked. "There seems to be a bit of a stir going on."

"Not much," her father sighed, thanking her as he took the mug of tea. "It appears some of the people visiting the park here had their tents ransacked while they were off on a tour."

Elizabeth gasped. "Was anything taken?"

Her father nodded. "Yes, but that's the odd thing. It was food and blankets, only. Rebecca, nothing of ours is gone?"

"Not that I saw," her mother replied, twisting her hands together. "How dreadful. Could it have been an animal?"

"I'm not sure," her father said. "But, I've been assured that we aren't in any danger. They are increasing the number of rangers in the park, and several will be on watch throughout the night."

"Goodness," her mother whispered. Then she smiled at Elizabeth. "A bit of excitement to write Robbie about, yes?"

"Yes," Elizabeth answered, realizing that she hadn't written to Robbie at all since they arrived. In fact, she hadn't had any desire to do so. What did that mean?

She spotted Kyle in the distance. "I see our guide. Let me see if he has any more news," she said, and hurried toward him.

Kyle's long legs were carrying him away, so Elizabeth called, "Kyle! Wait! Please!"

He turned, and the questioning look fell from his face, turning into a smile. "Elizabeth. What can I help you with?"

She felt flustered, and tried not to show it. "Papa was just telling me about the thefts," she said.

"Yes." A cloud came over his expression.

"I know something's going on. Something more than what he was told," she said. "Do you think it was one of the people who still live at the park?"

"No." He shook his head. "The few I met were the kindest and most honest folks alive. They also don't want to leave. They wouldn't do a thing to jeopardize that."

"Then you have an idea who it is?" Elizabeth asked.

"No," he told her, "but I can assure you that you aren't in any danger. We're watching over all the visitors."

Elizabeth took a deep breath. "I don't care about that. I want to know that you'll be safe."

"Me?" He looked at her in surprise.

"Yes, you. Is that so hard to believe?"

"Well, a little," he admitted.

"Why?" she asked.

"Because..." He furrowed his brow. "Well, it's my job. I knew what I signed up for."

"So I can't be concerned about your welfare?" Elizabeth asked.

Multiple expressions flickered over his face, and he stammered, but nothing coherent came out. After waiting for a moment, Elizabeth crossed her arms. "You're going to make me say it. That I like you. More than like you. And that's why I'm worried and don't want anything to happen to you."

His face turned red and then pale, as he whispered, "Elizabeth, I—"

"Never mind," she said, as a part of her soul withered. "I can see from your face you don't feel the same. It was my mistake." She turned on her heel.

Elizabeth's throat felt tight, and she fought back the urge to sniffle. She'd been so foolish, telling him how she'd felt. How had she not realized he was nothing more than polite? All of those moments she'd thought they shared were just in her imagination. Like it had been with Robbie.

A walk was what she needed. Time alone, so if more tears escaped, no one would know. Elizabeth hurried along the path, but she'd only gone maybe a dozen paces when she realized she was a little disoriented. She hesitated, not sure where she was. The path she thought would be before her wasn't. She plunged forward anyway, not wanting to see Kyle or admit that she was turned around.

"Wait, Elizabeth!" Kyle said, jogging after her. "That's not the right way. You can't go there."

"Let me go," Elizabeth said, hoping the tears that wanted to release from her embarrassment wouldn't. "Leave me alone. I'll find my way back."

"Stop. Please. I'm not mad at you. Just don't go in the woods," Kyle said, holding up his hands slowly. "It's dangerous."

"Why?" she asked. "Why won't you tell me? I'm not a child! I should know."

"We don't want anyone to panic," Kyle said. "We don't know who is behind this. But only taking food? Blankets? That's for survival, Elizabeth. Which means the person may be dangerous. I don't want you hurt. Please, don't wander off."

"If I do," Elizabeth asked, "would you follow me?"

"Yes," he said, "without hesitation."

"Why?" she whispered, wanting, hoping to hear what she longed for. Not words that would crush her heart.

"Because I like you," he told her, his eyes nearly blazing into her face. "More than like you. I shouldn't, but I do."

There was the unmistakable cocking of a gun just then, and Elizabeth let out a shriek as a man, dressed fully in a ranger uniform, showed himself from behind a large tree. He held a hand gun, and it was pointed right at Elizabeth.

"Don't move," the man said. "I've heard all I need to know. This little rich girl is going to be a fine ransom. Even better, her boyfriend is a ranger. You'll do whatever I tell you to."

"I'm not rich," Elizabeth protested, though she knew it might be futile. "And he's not my boyfriend."

"Got a private guide, don't you?" the man sniggered. "That means you've got money. And I'm pretty sure he just said he liked you."

"Let us go," Elizabeth whispered, not even able to hear herself over the thudding of her heart banging in her ears. "We won't tell anyone you're here."

"Sorry, sweetheart," the man said, "you're my little insurance policy."

"Take me instead," Kyle said, stepping closer. "Leave her alone."

"Stop right there," the man warned, "or I'll shoot her."

Kyle froze. His eyes flickered between hers and the man standing behind her. Elizabeth's chest tightened. She could see the man slightly, in her peripheral vision, and he appeared the sort to mean every word he said.

"Good. Very good. Now listen, this is what you're going to do," the man said, his voice calm, cold. "In three days, I'll send word to the ranger station and tell you where to find us. I won't hurt her before then. In the meantime, I want fifty thousand dollars. In cash. Or I'll kill her."

"Papa doesn't have that kind of money," Elizabeth gasped.

The hand around her tightened. "Maybe not, but the government does. Someone will find it, or they'll find your body and a whole lotta bad press. Now, run along, ranger boy."

"Why would you do this?" Elizabeth asked. "You're a park ranger. You're supposed to help people!"

"No, he's not," Kyle said, his eyes hard. "He's no ranger. You stole the uniform. That's Mason's number."

"And your little girlfriend here is lucky I stole some food too, else she'd starve." He took a half step closer to Elizabeth. "Now, get going. Don't turn around, or I'll shoot her."

Kyle stood, frozen. Elizabeth shivered, but managed to say, "It's okay. I'll be fine."

"I'll find you," Kyle said, his words a promise to them both.

"Unlikely," the man snorted.

At the same time, Elizabeth said, "I know you will."

Kyle stepped backward, slowly. Elizabeth could tell he didn't want to go. Anger flashed in his eyes, along with something she didn't want to see. Fear.

"Go," she pleaded, scared if he didn't the man would shoot him. "Go."

He nodded once, and turned, but stopped. Once more, he said, "I will find you."

And then he was gone.

Chapter 10

The hardest thing Kyle had ever done in his life had to be leaving Elizabeth there, a weapon pointed at her, and fear in her eyes.

Kyle sprinted back to where her parents were. He'd failed her. Failed them. But he meant just what he'd said. He would find her. Hopefully, it would be before even a single hair was harmed.

As he rushed up to the Lawrence family's tent, he glanced around. Where were they? He had to tell them and the head ranger. They had to search for her. Now. And, get the ransom started. Even if it wasn't going to be paid—he would find her before three days—in case they were being watched by another person, he had to do the motions.

"My boy," Mr. Lawrence said in his friendly voice. "You look shaken."

"Elizabeth has been kidnapped," Kyle said, wasting no time.

It was a punch to his stomach, seeing the man's expression turn to one of shock, then fear, then anguish. "My Elizabeth? What happened?" he asked sternly, even as his hands trembled as he crossed his arms.

"We were talking. She stepped onto one of the side trails that's closed. I asked her to come back. She was angry at me, thinking I knew more about the thefts than I was telling her. I think she got turned around." Kyle gestured in the direction it had happened.

"Sounds like my daughter," her father said. "And likely too proud to admit it. And she went further?"

"Not by much. I didn't want anything to happen to her," Kyle said. And then his voice cracked. "But it did. A man came from behind a tree. He was wearing a ranger uniform. But he wasn't a ranger. He held a gun to her."

Mr. Lawrence blinked a few times, and drew in a deep breath. "What next?"

Kyle realized he was shaking. Was it fear? Anger? Panic? He wasn't sure. "He said he wouldn't hurt her. For three days. He was going to hold her, for a ransom."

"How much?" Mr. Lawrence asked.

"Fifty thousand."

Mrs. Lawrence came out from the tent just then, her face pale. "Am I hearing what I think I am?" she asked.

"I'm sorry," Kyle said as he turned to her. "This is all my fault. I shouldn't have even let her put one foot on the trail. I wanted to attack him or follow her. But he had a gun and said if I did, he'd kill her. She told me to come get you. I knew I had to, but I wish more than anything I'd gone after her. Please, believe me."

"It's not your fault," Mr. Lawrence said. "You've done the right thing." He was quiet for a moment, his only movement wrapping an arm around his wife, who was trembling but quiet. He seemed to have recovered from his initial shock.

"I need to tell the other rangers," Kyle said.

"We will go with you," Mr. Lawrence said.

"It's possible the man doesn't even want the money," Mrs. Lawrence said as they quickly left the campsite. "He may be trying to cause problems for the park and prevent people from coming."

"That's true," Kyle said. "It wouldn't be the first time such a thing has happened." He led them toward the ranger station, then stopped, meeting their eyes in turn. "I will find her. I promise you that."

"We know you will," Mrs. Lawrence said. "You have our trust."

"I'm just sorry I've failed you in keeping her from this," Kyle said, his voice low.

"My boy," Mr. Lawrence said, putting his hand on Kyle's shoulder, "had you not been there, and she'd gotten turned around, right now, none of us would have known what happened. She could be hurt or worse, and we'd never know."

"You're so calm, so practical," Kyle said, jamming a hand through his hair. "How?"

Her parents exchanged a look, then Mrs. Lawrence put a hand on his arm, squeezing gently. "We just know, somehow, that you will find her, safe and sound."

"How?" he asked again, in desperation.

"Because," Mr. Lawrence said, "I see before me a man who isn't going to give up until he finds her."

"I won't," Kyle said, determination filling him, and turned back on the path, leading them to the ranger station.

Jeffs was there, and looked up in surprise as Kyle entered with Elizabeth's parents. Two other rangers were there as well, and as Kyle explained again what had happened, giving a description of the man who'd taken her, and every other detail he could remember, the rangers immediately sprang into action.

Jeffs ran to let the head ranger know. Ranger Peters, the youngest of the park rangers, set the Lawrences in a corner area with chairs and something to drink, while he got a description of Elizabeth. Ranger Lees set to scouring their roster for the best trackers.

Kyle knew everyone would be looking for her, quietly though, so as not to upset the park visitors or alert the kidnapper that they were searching for her.

"I will be searching too," Kyle told Jeffs when he returned to the station with a radio to connect him to the head ranger.

"We're going in threes," Jeffs said.

"I'd be faster and more silent alone," Kyle said.

"You can't. It's too dangerous," Jeffs told him.

"I'm responsible for her safety," Kyle argued. "Every delay means they are further away."

"I can't let you," Jeffs said, crossing his arms. "You know that."

"Then, he'll go with me," Mr. Lawrence said. "I need to search for my daughter. You wouldn't stop me, would you? I hired Kyle as my guide. This is my daughter. It's a father's right to search for her."

Jeffs hesitated, and the expression on his face was one of indecision. Finally, he said, "No, sir. I guess I can't stop you. But I can't provide you with anything other than a wish for good luck."

Mr. Lawrence nodded. "Understood." He turned to his wife. "Stay here."

"Bring her back," she said, looking at Kyle. He nodded, and quickly walked out of the building with Mr. Lawrence.

Once a few steps away, the other man stopped and said, "I can't go with you. I'd slow you down and be too noisy. I will be reaching out to a few of my contacts and see who can help and in what capacity. I will also make sure that the park superintendent, Superintendent Lassiter, is aware of what's happened. Go. But be careful."

"I will," Kyle promised, and hurried toward the last place he'd seen Elizabeth. There, on the trail, fear in her eyes and a weapon pressed against her side.

Despite what the man had said about not hurting her for three days, Kyle didn't trust him. He just prayed he wouldn't be too late to rescue her.

Chapter 11

Elizabeth tried to keep up as the man half dragged her through the forest.

"Be quiet," he hissed once more.

"I can't help it," she said, nearly in tears as he yanked on her wrist. "We're going too fast. I can't help but be noisy because you aren't letting me watch where I'm going." Just then, she tripped over a tree root, almost as if to prove her point.

He snarled, but slowed down slightly, and Elizabeth walked more quietly. Truthfully, she had been making more noise than she needed to most of their trek. The reason for that was if someone else was around, perhaps they'd see her or hear her and come to her aid.

Soon, the sun would start to set. Elizabeth had learned that the tall and dense trees made it dark sooner. That scared her. But at the same time, if she could convince her kidnapper to make a campfire, maybe the smoke and the light could lead Kyle to her.

She trusted him when he said he'd find her. The knowledge, and the look in his eyes as he'd said it so fiercely, stayed in her mind, and comforted her as her feet started to hurt and her hands became scratched from branches. Even parts of her legs where her dress got caught on branches were scraped and stung.

Her kidnapper paused and glanced around, as if trying to decide which direction to go. Elizabeth took the opportunity to lean against a tree. It wasn't for rest, though. Her fingernails dug into the bark and she tried to wriggle some of it away. She knew she shouldn't. The tree needed it. But she needed to leave Kyle a sign even more.

"This way," the man said, pointing.

"Can I just have one moment to rest?" Elizabeth pleaded. As he glared at her, she dropped her eyes and whispered, "It's just you are so tall and strong. I'm so much smaller and weaker. I'm having a hard time keeping up."

He thought that over for a moment, then nodded. "Five minutes, nothing more," he told her. "We want to get there before dark."

Elizabeth nodded, and when he wasn't looking, tried to scratch an E into the spot she'd pulled away the bark, along with an arrow. As she was pulled away again, she glanced backward. It wasn't much and it wasn't very good, but if someone was searching for her, perhaps they'd spot it.

She wished she had something she could drop to make a little trail, but she didn't have anything. Not even the necklace she often wore. She'd left the beaded strand in her tent, not wanting it to catch and break. Now, she'd give most anything to be wearing it, and use the bright red beads to make a trail of breadcrumbs.

Elizabeth's steps slowed, but this time she wasn't pretending. She was exhausted, and thirsty, and anxious to rest. How long had they been walking? She wasn't sure, but it had felt as though they were going in circles. Was that deliberate? A way to throw off their trail for someone who was searching for them?

Just as she felt like her legs couldn't carry her much further, they came upon a small log cabin. Her kidnapper opened the door, then pointed inside. Elizabeth went in, and he followed her, locking the door behind them.

"Is this your house?" Elizabeth asked, as she looked around.

"No," he said. "But this is where we are staying."

She didn't answer, just did a slow turn. The inside was nearly empty, though there was a single wooden bench and a chair with a broken back. It was obvious the man had been in there recently, as ash was in the fireplace, and a faint smell of smoke filled the room.

"Get comfortable." The man laughed. He went to a sack in the corner and pulled out an apple and a sandwich. "Here you go. Dinner."

Elizabeth took it and ate slowly. Who knew when he'd feed her again? And eating slowly helped to both pass time and keep her mind occupied. She counted each bite and tried to make them last.

When she was finished, she observed her kidnapper, studying him when he didn't notice. She'd only gotten short glimpses while they were walking. Medium height and build, dirty blond hair, gray eyes. He hadn't shaved for at least a week, and smelled like he'd not been friends with a bar of soap for a while. Though the uniform had misled her at first into thinking he was a park ranger, the longer she was around him, the more she wondered how she could have thought that.

The man stretched out in front of the only door. He yawned, and said, "There's a covered bucket in the corner if you need to use it. Meantime, we wait."

Her eyes wide, Elizabeth looked where he indicated, then looked away again. She knew at some point she'd have to use it, but hoped it would be only when the man was asleep or not nearby. Her cheeks flamed at the idea.

Kyle, please find me, and hurry.

But as soon as she thought it, Elizabeth remembered how she'd been angry at him. What had he thought of her? Possibly that she was spoiled. If only she'd listened to him and not stepped on that path. But she'd been upset. Hurt. And felt so humiliated.

Here, she'd thought that there was something starting to grow between them. Was there? She'd been so hot from her anger she had trouble hearing. Had he said he liked her? The moment had happened so fast, hardly a blink and a breath before her kidnapper appeared. Elizabeth wondered if she'd just imagined it.

Where was Kyle right now? He'd tell her parents and the other park rangers, she was sure about that, but Elizabeth wasn't sure he personally would find her.

If I ever see him again, she thought, *I'm going to apologize. And then, I'll go home and make do with Robbie. Not that he'd want me. Robbie never wanted me. So, maybe I'll just be alone. I'll forget all about how Kyle made me feel important, as though I mattered. As though he cared about what I had to say. He was only doing it because that was his job. I see that now. Even if he said he liked me, I imagine it was just as a friend.*

Her heart sank and her stomach hurt. Not from the food, but from the despair filling her. Was this a broken heart? She'd never really had one, so she wasn't sure.

There was a tiny crack in the boards that covered the single window of the cabin. Elizabeth moved toward it, and stared through. Darkness had fallen, and she felt sure it was near her bedtime. The inside of the cabin, lit only by a single candle that was guttering, felt scary.

Elizabeth sank to the floor, pulling her knees up to her chin and resting her head on them. Her eyes stayed fixed on the scrap of moonlight that shone through the crack.

Never in her life had she ever felt so alone. She knew she couldn't count on Kyle or anyone else to find her. She was going to have to figure out how to escape on her own. But how? And once she did, because Elizabeth refused to believe she couldn't, how would she find her way back? All of the trails looked the same, and the park was so large.

Her kidnapper let out a loud snore, causing Elizabeth to startle. She pulled herself further in the corner and leaned against the wall. It would be hard, but she needed to rest. Who knew what tomorrow would bring? And she'd need every bit of her strength to escape.

Chapter 12

They had too much of a head start. That was the only thing Kyle could think to himself as he picked his way through the forest, searching for tracks. The last he'd seen, they were at the side of the trail. It made sense, didn't it, to not take the trail? The path would be quicker but also easier to be spotted on. Hence him now carefully walking through the woods, trying both not to make noise and not miss a sign.

He'd been walking for about an hour. In truth, he had no idea if he was even going the right way. He had no firm evidence. He did, however, have a gut feeling. And since that was all he had, he was going with it.

It was getting much darker. He had a small flashlight, but didn't want to use it. It was there in an emergency, but if he could avoid using it, then he'd limit the chance of the kidnapper seeing it and potentially hurting Elizabeth.

He knew the man had said he wouldn't—for three days. But how could he trust someone who would kidnap another? He was already a thief, and impersonating a park ranger. How long had he been walking among them? Watching, seeing routines, stealing? Had he kidnapped anyone else?

The idea filled him with more worry, and he wished he'd thought of it sooner, so that the others could be looking into that possibility.

Kyle glanced up. The moon was rising, and was faint between the trees' branches. Every now and then, it filtered through, illuminating a spot.

He squinted. Like it did now...on a tree where the bark had been recently peeled away. It was human done, not nature, he could tell. Kyle's heart quickened, and he ran his hand over the spot. There was something scratched there, but he couldn't see what. It was too dark.

He pulled the flashlight from his pocket and shined it on the spot the bark had been pulled from. There was a sloppily scratched-in E, with an arrow. Kyle flicked off the flashlight, and rested his hand on the symbol.

"Thank you," he whispered. "Please, hold on a little longer."

It helped, knowing he was on the right path, but the problem was the national park was just under 200,000 acres.

"But they only had about an hour's head start." Kyle looked around, trying to calculate how much further that was. "They wouldn't be walking still, in the dark." He tapped the tree with his fingers. "And now and again, I saw deep tracks, and a good number of broken twigs, as though someone were walking slowly, heavily. Maybe Elizabeth was doing that on purpose. Trying to move slowly."

Kyle started in the direction of the arrow. He glanced up at the moon. And completely missed the small fallen tree. It was enough to jar him as he tripped, and a searing sensation tore through his injured leg, burning with an intensity that had him gasping and tears coming to his eyes.

Righting himself, Kyle hobbled to a larger tree and leaned against it, trying to hold in the pain that wanted to escape verbally. He forced himself to take several deep breaths. Eventually, the pain subsided, leaving him with a dull ache instead of the red, hot poker stabbing he'd felt.

"That's going to set the healing back a little," Kyle groaned quietly, rubbing at his hip and leg.

No matter. His pain was the least of his concern right now. Rescuing Elizabeth was all he could think about.

Moonlight revealed a shadow the size of a small building looming in the distance, and Kyle quickened his pace, as much as he felt able to. He'd been lucky not to break his foot or wrist when he'd fallen earlier, and he didn't want to risk another accident.

Slowly, as quietly as he could, Kyle approached the cabin. It might have been one that one of the former residents lived in. The cabin's door was closed, and the small window didn't give any light. He crept close, and peered into the house from the window's edge. He didn't see any movement inside. But that was because he couldn't see anything at all. The window was mostly boarded, and all he had to work with was a small crack.

Gently, Kyle wiggled at the board on the window. It would come loose if he worked on it. That was something, at least, but he decided to try the door first.

Kyle put his hand on the door's latch and pushed slightly. It was locked. He went back to the window, and listened closely. He couldn't hear anything but the rustling of the tree leaves. Deciding to risk it, Kyle pried off the board as quietly as he could, then turned on his flashlight and held it to the window's glass. He moved it around and peered in.

It was an empty cabin. Nothing was inside. Frustration filled him. He thought maybe he'd found them. Kyle started to turn away, then stopped. What if she had been here? Had left another clue? It would be wise to check.

He tried the door again, pushing hard with his shoulder. It opened just enough for him to slip his hand inside and lift the small latch that had locked it from within.

Flashlight in hand, Kyle entered, and sniffed. Woodsmoke. It was recent. A day, maybe. He went to the fireplace and checked the ashes. Cold. But recent. Maybe the kidnapper had been here. Before he'd taken Elizabeth.

Slowly, he moved the light around the room hoping to see something. Anything. Then he froze. In the corner of the room was an apple core. He moved closer to it. It was fresh. Browning, but not rotten. It was from today. But the most important thing, was right next to it, was another scratched-in E.

Kyle let his fingers trace over it. She had *been* here. But where was she at now? How could he find her? Was it better to wait for daylight? Go back and get help? He didn't want to do either. He wanted to find her. Rescue her. Protect her.

"But I don't know where you are," he whispered. "Elizabeth, where are you?"

As though she'd tell him, Kyle held still, waiting and holding his breath, not even daring to breathe and miss a hint of sound, but none came.

He left the cabin, and stood at the front, feeling indecisive as to which way he should go. Forward? Left? Right? Kyle closed his eyes and focused on where his instinct said, then moved in that direction.

It had to be after midnight by now. He was getting tired, and his hip still throbbed, but that didn't matter. Neither did the fact he was thirsty.

Elizabeth was here, somewhere. And he was going to find her.

Chapter 13

"Get up. We're leaving."

"Huh?" Elizabeth rubbed the sleep from her eyes. She must have dozed off.

"You heard me. We're going. Moving to another place. Further off the path."

"Why?" she asked groggily.

"Because I say so," he growled, grabbing the sack of food. "Hurry up. Meet me outside in two minutes. That gives you time to use the bucket if you need to."

Elizabeth shivered and scrambled to her feet, humiliation warring with practicality. As soon as the door shut, she hurried to the bucket, and she glanced around the room. She'd hoped to stay, hoped that Kyle would find them.

Though it was almost futile—how unlikely was it that he'd stumble across this cabin?—there had to be a way to leave a sign that she had been there. Her gaze fell on the apple core. That was it! Even if he didn't find this place until tomorrow, it should still be fresh, not withered away.

"Thirty seconds," the kidnapper called through the cabin door.

Elizabeth scratched an E as quickly as she could into the cabin floor, and then set the apple core next to it. It wasn't much, but it was all she could do.

Just as the cabin door swung open, she was inches away. "I'm here," she said, stepping out into the night.

"This way," he grunted, and set off, the gun in one hand and pointed toward her, the food in the other.

"I'm not going to run away," Elizabeth promised. "Where would I go? I'm safer with you. There are wild animals out here, and you have a gun. But you don't have to point it at me."

"I can do anything I want," he smirked. "Already have."

"Can I ask your name?" Elizabeth asked. "You already know mine. It seems it would be only fair, since we are going to be acquainted for a few days."

He was quiet for a moment, then answered, "Ed. You can call me Ed."

"Ed. Thank you," Elizabeth told him, hoping if she was polite, he might feel guilty and let her go.

He just grunted, and motioned her to go ahead of him with the gun. So much for him putting it away.

As they continued in the dark, the moon mostly hidden by the trees, Elizabeth tried not to feel scared. Rustling in the forest could have been just leaves. But it could have been bears or mountain lions or any other manner of predators they'd been warned were there. She hadn't been lying about it being safer to be with him if they were in the open. He did have a gun, and that was some protection, as he surely wouldn't want himself to be hurt by an animal either.

They trudged through the woods for almost an hour, and came to another abandoned cabin. Ed let them in, and Elizabeth was surprised to see this one was slightly more homey inside. She wondered if it had belonged to one of the displaced families or if Ed had been making this his home. He lit a small candle that flickered dimly, but provided just a little light to see by.

There was a large pot over the fireplace, and in addition to a few chairs was a pallet with blankets. Ed pulled off one of the blankets and offered it to her, on his way to lie down in front of the door, blocking her way out.

Elizabeth had accepted it gingerly, trying not to be too disgusted at the thought of wondering when the last time was that the blanket had been washed. She carried it to a corner of the room and folded it, then lay down, her back to the wall.

This cabin was a little larger, but still only had one way in or out, though there were two small boarded-up windows.

"Ed?" Elizabeth asked, her voice sounding very small in the dark.

"What?"

"Are you going to kill me?"

The longer the silence stretched, the more Elizabeth filled with terror. Why wouldn't he answer? It either meant that yes, he was planning to or no, he didn't think he could go through with it. She hoped it was the latter, but didn't want to upset him by pressing. She just wanted to know.

"It's okay," she finally whispered. "You don't have to tell me. Just...can you promise to let my parents know I love them? And I really did try to be a good daughter?"

Heavy silence filled the room, and he finally answered. "I will. But I'm hoping it doesn't come to that."

"I'm hoping too," Elizabeth said, her voice choking.

"It all depends on if they pay up, girlie," he told her. In the near dark, their eyes met. "I'm not wanting to hurt you. But I will. Sometimes that's the only way to get someone to listen to you."

"What is it you are trying to say that you feel isn't being heard?" Elizabeth asked. "Maybe I can help."

"What would you know about anything? You live a privileged life," the man sneered. "All you people here do.

Don't have to worry about your next meal or finding work when there isn't any."

"Is that what this is about?" Elizabeth asked. "You need the money because you can't find a job?"

"Used to have one," he told her. "Catching animals, selling their meat, selling their hides. But the park came along, see? Can't do that anymore. The land is theirs, they say."

"Is there something else you want to do?" Elizabeth asked.

"You assume I wanted to do that in the first place," Ed said.

"Then do something else," Elizabeth told him. She sat up. "You can be or do whatever you want. No one gets to choose for you. Start over, somewhere fresh."

"That's what the fifty grand is for," Ed told her. "Getting a new start. Setting up proper."

Elizabeth was quiet. Finally, she said, "I hope that you get to start over. But I also really hope you don't kill me. I just want to go home."

"As long as your boyfriend doesn't come rushing after you and your folks pay up, you'll make it out fine," he told her. "Now get some sleep."

"He's not my boyfriend," Elizabeth said, then lay back down.

"Sure, sure," the man laughed. "Don't nobody look at a woman like that if he doesn't love her."

Elizabeth didn't know what to say. Ed propped himself up on his elbow. "Prove it, then. If he's not your boyfriend, come over here, next to me. Convince me."

She shrank back further against the wall, while Ed threw his head back and laughed. Soon, his chuckles turned into mumbles, as he talked to himself. Curled into a ball, Elizabeth wrapped her arms around herself tightly. How exactly had Kyle been looking at her? It was just a look, wasn't it?

But it hadn't been. She hadn't been wrong. There was something she'd felt—and it seemed that Kyle had not only felt it, but someone else saw he had. What did that mean? Probably nothing. Maybe her father had that kind of money, Elizabeth didn't know, but she doubted it. Her father worked hard. They lived in a small, simple home. She didn't have endless dresses or books or go to fancy parties. They were just...normal.

Perhaps to someone who couldn't get work or couldn't buy food, that did seem privileged. She didn't know. Her family had always helped anyone who needed it. That's just what they did, and right now she was very torn between her desire for survival, and doing whatever it took to stay alive, and feeling sympathy for the man, wondering if she could help him in some way.

But none of that mattered, not really. Ed was going to do whatever he thought he needed to do. And Elizabeth had never felt so alone in her entire life.

Chapter 14

Even though it was the middle of the night, Kyle pressed on. His exhaustion and the ache that still filled his hip was nothing compared to the burning desire to find Elizabeth. He had no idea if the other rangers were still out there looking for her, or if they'd stopped and gone back for some rest, but he knew he wasn't going to stop.

Nothing was going to keep him from finding her. It didn't matter it was almost like looking for a grain of salt in the sugar jar, he wasn't going to stop until he'd combed every inch of the park.

He was on the right trail. That he knew. Even if he wasn't sure how he knew it, he had to trust in that feeling that filled him. It didn't matter it was senseless. Intuition based. Not the least bit factual. He had to find her. Had to protect her. And he would. He had promised her and her parents.

A low rumble of thunder filled the air. A storm might be approaching. That wasn't good. With the shape of the valley, sometimes storms circled around them. Other times, they lingered, almost trapped in the mountains. Hopefully, this would go past them. Rain would make it much more difficult to find her. It also made the likelihood of only him searching for her a near reality. It was dangerous to be in these woods during a storm with lightning.

Kyle had to use his flashlight now, when the clouds grew thicker and blotted out the moon. He kept it pointed low, hoping that the beam of light wouldn't alert anyone that he was nearby. He also didn't want to attract any biting insects, or larger creatures who were curious—and hungry.

The forest looked different in the dark, but Kyle had the feeling he'd been here before. In fact...if he remembered correctly, there was a small homestead ahead. It would be abandoned, if it was still standing. Perhaps Elizabeth's kidnapper had taken shelter there with her. If nothing else, and it was abandoned, if the rain started suddenly, he could stop and wait it out.

It was a good plan, and he hurried forward. Not a moment later, Kyle spotted the low wall made from large rocks. That meant he was entering that particular land parcel. He turned off his flashlight, both to save the battery and to conceal his approach, and crouched behind the wall, only rising up enough to take in the cabin before him. Larger than the last, though not by much, it looked quiet. Empty.

But then, through a crack in a board covering a window, he saw a glint of light.

Kyle slowly crept forward. He imagined the door was locked from the inside. There wouldn't be any other way in but through a window, unless he could get the door opened from the inside.

He pressed his eye to the sliver of the opening, trying to see as much as he could. From that small view, all he saw was the candle, and a few chairs. But he could hear voices.

Frustrated at the low, muffled sound, he moved as quietly as he could to the front door and pressed his ear closer.

"You know, sweetheart," a man's voice said, "I've decided."

"Decided on what?" Elizabeth's trembling voice asked.

Excitement filled Kyle. He'd found her! Now, he just had to get her out of there. She sounded scared, and he didn't want to wait any longer to see what happened. He glanced around for something he could use as a weapon to defend her and himself. Nothing struck him as being able to block a bullet. He'd have to be careful. His mind worked furiously to come up with a plan.

Kyle tensed as the kidnapper answered. "I'm going to keep you, and the money."

"But you promised you'd let me go," Elizabeth said, her voice shrill and panicked.

Panic surged in Kyle as well. There was no time to do anything but act.

"I changed my mind. You're too pretty. Smell too sweet. Don't worry, sweetheart, you'll get used to me. I'm not half bad once I'm cleaned up."

"Stay away from me," Elizabeth said firmly, her voice fainter.

Was she backing away? Was he about to touch her? Harm her?

Kyle did the only thing he could think to do. He knocked on the door, and then hid around the side.

The cabin door opened suddenly, just a few inches. Kyle stood patiently, biding his time. He knew if he waited long enough, the man would either step through the door or shut it. If he closed the door, he'd knock again. At some point, he'd have to step through to see who was outside, and Kyle would be ready.

Time seemed to slow. Finally, the door opened a little wider. Then wider. A man stepped out, glancing around. "Who is it?" he asked.

Quick as he could, Kyle sprang up from where he'd been crouching, and hit the kidnapper on the back of his head with his metal flashlight. "Park ranger," he said. "You're under arrest."

The kidnapper fell to a heap at Kyle's feet. Kyle didn't let his guard down in case it was a ruse. He stepped back, ready to knock the man out cold, if the first time hadn't worked. When the criminal didn't move, Kyle cautiously inched closer.

Elizabeth came to the door just then. "Kyle?" she asked, her voice filled with surprise and relief.

"It's me," he told her.

At his words, lightning streaked across the sky, and rain began to fall. Kyle grabbed the man's arms and started to drag him into the cabin. "We aren't going anywhere until the rain stops, and it's light out," he told her. "We need to wait too, for him to wake up. I'm not carrying him back. Is there anything we can tie him up with?"

"I'll look," Elizabeth said.

Kyle took the man's gun. He considered keeping it with him, but what if the man somehow wrestled it away from him, turned it on Elizabeth again? He couldn't chance it. Both he and the criminal knew he wouldn't risk her life. He'd put it out of the man's sight, but not out of his.

Glancing around, Kyle set the gun on a shelf built into the wall, then returned his flashlight to his pocket. He looked down at the kidnapper, who was still out cold.

"Will this work?" Elizabeth held out some cords of various lengths.

"It will have to," Kyle said. He tied the shorter pieces together, then tied the man's hands together behind his back. "I'd like something for his feet too," he said, glancing around. "I hate to do it, but I'm going to cut one of the blankets into strips."

"I can do it," Elizabeth said. "Do you have a pocket knife?"

Kyle nodded, and handed it to her. He wanted to ask her how she was. Look her over for himself, but this needed to come first. The kidnapper was dangerous, possibly far more than either of them realized, and any delay in getting him bound might cause an injury to Elizabeth or himself.

A few moments later, when the kidnapper was securely tied and in the corner of the room, Kyle finally turned to her, stepping forward cautiously.

"Are you...are you okay?"

To his surprise, Elizabeth threw herself into his arms. "I'm so glad to see you," she said, her face buried in his chest. "How did you find me?"

"I don't know," he told her. "Just...kept feeling a pull in this direction. I did find the E scratched into the tree. And the one by the apple. Those were good clues," he told her.

"I'm glad it worked," she told him, still against his chest. "I was so scared. And I'm so sorry. I should have listened to you, and not gone on that path."

"I didn't mean to upset you," Kyle said, letting one hand stroke her back. "It's just I knew someone was lurking. I didn't expect him to be right there, though. You've no idea how angry I am at myself."

"You shouldn't be," Elizabeth said. She glanced up at him, her cheeks damp with tears. "Do my parents know?"

"Yes. Your father actually helped me to get away to look for you."

She smiled. "That sounds like Papa. He doesn't always care for all of the proper channels things have to go through and how much time it can take. Unnecessary, he calls it. He also really seems to like you."

"I like him too," Kyle said, resting his cheek on the top of her soft head. "I like all of you. You the most, though."

She gave a soft laugh, but didn't let go of him. Kyle didn't mind. He'd stand like this forever, if Elizabeth could be in his arms.

The sudden sound of rain pounding on the roof made them both look up.

"I hope it won't leak," Elizabeth said.

"I hope not too," Kyle agreed. He led her over to a chair. "Do you want to tell me everything that happened?"

She nodded. "That's a good idea. Just in case I forget something." She hesitated, "I tried to be nice to Ed, thinking maybe he'd feel sorry for what he did and let me go. Maybe that gave him the wrong idea. I certainly wasn't leading him on."

"Ed?" Kyle pointed his thumb to the kidnapper.

"Yes."

Elizabeth went on to explain what had happened since the man took her. Kyle was relieved that she hadn't been hurt, and he'd gotten there just in time. From the sound of things, even though Elizabeth was skirting around the moments before he'd arrived, it sounded like the man was about to get too familiar with her.

The idea made him furious, and he couldn't wait to get the man back to the ranger station. Once it was light out, it would be much easier to find their way back, and they would also be able to move quicker through the dense trees and brush. Using the trail would definitely speed things up, once they were able to find one. With any luck, they'd run across a few other rangers, and they'd take the kidnapper back for him.

Kyle didn't want to stare at him a moment longer than he had to, and he wanted to spare Elizabeth any more mental and physical anguish from being around the man.

Soon, Elizabeth started to yawn, and moved down to the floor. Kyle wrapped a blanket around her shoulders, and she leaned against his shoulder. "Don't leave," she whispered, as her eyes drooped. "Please."

"I'm right here," Kyle said softly, wrapping an arm around her. He held her close, and even though he thought she might have fallen asleep, he added, "I'm not going to let anything happen to you."

The rain pounding outside, Elizabeth safe in his arms, and the fact the kidnapper was still knocked out and securely tied allowed Kyle to rest, and he drifted off, thinking to himself that he'd never felt as content as he did right now, with Elizabeth in his arms.

Chapter 15

It was sometime before dawn that Elizabeth stirred, wondering why her neck and back felt stiff. Her arms and legs stung, as though she'd been cut a dozen times over. Then it all rushed back.

The kidnapping. Walking through the woods. The first cabin. Moving again. The second one. Ed trying to kiss her. And then Kyle, rescuing her.

She'd fallen asleep against Kyle, his strong arm around her. It wasn't something she'd meant to do, but honestly, other than the ache on her backside from the hard floor, she wasn't sure she'd ever slept so well in her life.

As she moved slightly, Kyle's eyes opened instantly. "Are you all right?" he asked.

"I'm fine," Elizabeth said. She glanced over to where Ed sat, tied and scowling at them.

"You're awake," Kyle said flatly, walking toward the man.

Ed didn't answer.

"There's food in the bag," Elizabeth said, going over to the sack. As she stood, she peered through a crack in the boards covering the window. "And the rain has stopped. The sun will be out soon and we can go back."

Kyle joined her and rummaged through the bag where some whole fruits, a few cheese sandwiches, and some boxes of crackers sat.

"It's a good idea to eat something," Kyle said. He took out a sandwich, and dropped it near Ed. "Here. I'm not untying you. You'll have to make it work."

"Maybe you'll come feed me, sweetheart?" Ed smirked.

"Say anything else, and I'll gag you," Kyle warned.

Elizabeth helped herself to some of the crackers and an orange. "I feel a little bad eating someone else's food," she admitted.

"I'll find out who had supplies missing, and the rangers will replace it," Kyle assured her.

That made her feel a little better. She glanced over at Ed, who was leaning forward, chomping on the sandwich. When he caught her looking at him, he winked. Disgusted, she turned away.

She wished that Ed wasn't there. She wanted to talk to Kyle. Ask him if what he'd said about liking her was true. So much of the time she'd been held hostage, it was that idea and hope that kept her distracted from her terrible circumstance. If there was any possibility that they could have some sort of a future together... The question burned in her, and it was all she could do not to ask him. Part of her was afraid he'd say no, and could she blame him? He was a park ranger...she was a tourist. And, right now, a job. He likely had rules about that. Besides, how foolish was this? They hadn't known each other for long!

But things could change, couldn't they? People could get to know each other better with time. They actually might, if he got the job he was hoping for at the university there in Philadelphia.

How could she make that happen? Elizabeth could just imagine herself there, seeking him out after his job for the day was done. Leaving, her hand in his. Strolling through the parks. Listening to a concert together, her head on his shoulder. Just like she'd slept last night.

Just like she'd sat listening to music a few times with Robbie. Robbie. Elizabeth's heart sank. She didn't know what to do. She didn't feel this way at all about Robbie. But Virginia felt so far from Pennsylvania and Kyle. If he didn't move there...

But what if he did? What would she do then? Without some sort of an aforementioned plan between the two of them...

"Elizabeth?"

She looked up, startled. Kyle was kneeling next to her, a worried look on his face. "Are you okay?" he asked.

"Yes, yes," she answered in a rush. "I'm sorry. I got lost in some thoughts."

He nodded slowly. "I understand. There's something I want to talk with you about, myself." He glanced over at Ed, who was still working on his sandwich. "Just not with our present company."

She laughed softly. "I quite agree. I was thinking the same."

"I think we should get going. But, when we get back, after you've had time to reunite with your parents and answer any questions that law enforcement wants to ask, maybe we could go on a short walk. Just us. Not far away."

"I'd like that," Elizabeth whispered, looking up at him. "I like you, Kyle."

The words popped out of her mouth, though she'd not intended to speak them again. In for a penny, in for a pound, she figured, and continued, "And I don't want to leave here without knowing what might become of us. If you also like me, and want to try."

She bit her lip, worried about his reaction, but his serious eyes melted into warmth, and a smile twitched on his lips.

"I'd like that," Kyle told her, gently bringing one of his hands to her cheek.

"Awww, look at the lovebirds," Ed said, laughing cruelly. "You wouldn't still want her if you knew how she was throwing herself at me."

"That's it," Kyle said, springing to his feet, his eyes flashing with anger. "I told you to keep quiet."

Elizabeth watched as he cut a few more blanket strips and bound them around Ed's mouth. She wouldn't say it was a bad idea.

"Are you ready?" Kyle asked. "Once we start, I'll untie his feet."

She nodded, then asked, "Would you mind if I had just a second in the bushes?"

He looked confused, then his face colored at the understanding. "Go ahead. We'll wait here," he said. "There might actually be an outhouse." He opened the front door and looked, then pointed to a small building. "There. Watch for snakes as you go in."

Elizabeth nodded, and in a moment rejoined them. Ed's gun was tucked into Kyle's waistband, and he pushed Ed ahead of him, keeping a hand on the other man's shoulder.

"Are we very far?" Elizabeth asked.

"I think in about two hours we can get there," Kyle said. Then, he paused. "I wonder...I know there are others searching for you." He looked over at her. "I'm going to call for help. Cover your ears."

Nodding, Elizabeth did as he asked. Kyle raised the gun he'd taken from Ed into the air and fired a single shot. All around them, bushes rustled, from what she assumed to be wildlife hiding. Then, he took out a small whistle, and let out three loud, long blasts.

"Let's keep going," Kyle said. "That should get some attention. I'll do it again in about fifteen minutes."

"That's a good idea," Elizabeth said. "That should send people coming."

"I hope," he told her. "Then I'll get a little help with this one."

Ed was dragging his feet, just like Elizabeth had done the first night. He was deliberately showing down and veering. Was he trying to buy time for a friend to rescue him? The idea both alarmed and angered Elizabeth. Then, she noticed Kyle's limp. It was more pronounced than she'd ever seen it. He must have hurt himself coming after her.

Fury filled her toward Ed, and she stopped at a large, sturdy branch the size and thickness of a good walking stick. She picked it up and pushed it into Ed's back.

"You walk properly," she told him, "or I'll use this on you. And yes, I will. Don't test my patience. I want to get back, and you're moving too slowly. My father was a fencing champion and taught me some walking stick moves before we came. I'm eager to practice them."

She swished the stick a few times in exacting movements, sharp and clean and stopping just an inch from his knee, before sweeping it to his neck, again, stopping just before she made contact.

The anger in his eyes was unmistakable, but Ed walked properly. Elizabeth held the stick firmly, determined to use it if she needed to.

"That's impressive," Kyle said admiringly, and Elizabeth blushed.

"Not too unladylike?" she asked.

"Who cares about that? It was amazing. You're going to teach me that, I hope," he told her.

She couldn't stop the grin forming on her face, and it, along with a dose of excitement and hope, only grew when she heard three sharp whistles in the distance.

Kyle withdrew his own whistle and blasted on it again. He was answered, in at least two directions.

"They're close," Kyle said, nudging Ed forward.

Elizabeth hurried, the stick tight in her grasp. She wasn't convinced Ed wouldn't struggle or try to run for it. They hadn't gone much further before she could hear voices and shouts.

The next few moments were chaotic. They were surrounded by men in park ranger uniforms. She was given a blanket, and a medic sat her on a rock to do a quick examination. Ed was taken into a cluster of rangers and she no longer saw him. The speed at which it all happened seemed to blur one event into the next.

"Kyle?" she asked, trying to shrug off the medic before her. "Kyle?"

"I'm here," he told her, hurrying over.

"Your leg. Let him look at it," she pleaded.

"I'll be fine," Kyle said. "When we get back, I'll get looked at. We shouldn't delay. You need proper food and rest, and your parents are beyond worried about you, I'm sure."

"Don't worry, miss," the medic said. "I'll check him out thoroughly too."

She nodded, though unsatisfied. Elizabeth looked back over at the medic, who was checking her pulse. "I'm okay," she assured him. "Just tired. I'm ready to walk."

He nodded. "We're about an hour from your camp," he told her.

"That's fine," she said.

A half dozen park rangers went with them, and though Elizabeth walked next to Kyle, she felt an absence. They were no longer alone. When would they get that time to be together again?

As if he could sense her thoughts, Elizabeth felt his fingers brush against hers. She wanted to take his hand, not caring what others thought, but she couldn't. She didn't dare risk his job or his reputation.

Instead, she let her fingers squeeze his gently, then let go, trying to ignore the painful squeezing that echoed in her chest at the loss.

Chapter 16

The moment they reached the camp, Elizabeth was swept into her parents' embrace. Kyle tried to step back, to give them their privacy, as much as could be done considering the fact there were tourists, park rangers, law enforcement, and two medical personnel clustered near her. She was taken into the ranger station, and Kyle hesitated a moment outside, unsure of what he should do. Was he supposed to go in?

He was about to turn away, figuring someone would find him if he was needed, when Mr. Lawrence stopped him. "My boy," he said.

Kyle swallowed hard, unsure of the man's demeanor. His face was stern, and there was a muscle twitching in Mr. Lawrence's face.

"Yes, sir?"

"I...I can't thank you enough. I am indebted. How can I thank you? Is there a favor I can do for you?"

That hadn't been what Kyle expected to hear. He shook his head, and stammered, "No, no. Nothing. That's not expected. It's not why I did it. I still feel responsible, and—"

"You were not," Mr. Lawrence assured him, and then smiled. It was a warm smile, one that made Kyle feel so much better. "I knew I didn't make a mistake in asking for you."

That's right. Mr. Lawrence had asked for him. Kyle took a deep breath. "Sir, may I ask why you asked for me specifically?"

The older man studied him for a moment, then said, "I had a feeling, that's all. Do you ever get those?"

"Sometimes," Kyle said. "That's...that's how I found your daughter. I just went where I was feeling."

Mr. Lawrence nodded. "Then you understand."

But he didn't. Because Mr. Lawrence had asked for him before they'd even met. How had he known, all the way back home, in Pennsylvania, that he, Kyle Struggs, was there? Or even existed?

Elizabeth's father looked like he was about to say more, when Mrs. Lawrence stepped out of the ranger station, exhaustion etched on her face. "There you are," she said when she spotted her husband. And then she noticed Kyle, and before he could quite realize what was happening, she'd thrown her arms around him. "Thank you, my dear," she said on a sob. "Thank you."

Moisture came to Kyle's eyes, he wasn't sure why, and he simply nodded, unsure what to say, while Mr. Lawrence gently pulled his wife back.

"Elizabeth wants to finish the trip here," Mrs. Lawrence said. Her smile was a little watery. "So, will we see you tomorrow morning?"

"I'll be there," Kyle promised.

He watched as the Lawrences went back inside the ranger station, then went back to his dormitory to wash and change clothes. After a meal, the medic looked him over, and Jeffs stopped by to hear what had happened and take down his testimony. It wasn't even supper time yet, but Kyle was so exhausted he fell right to sleep, only waking up at dawn.

Oddly, the rest wasn't as good as when Elizabeth had been tucked up under his arm, a fact he noticed upon awakening, but that didn't matter. He hoped they'd have a chance to talk in private. That was unlikely, seeing as her parents wouldn't want to let her out of their sight, but they'd figure something out. He was sure of that.

On the walk to their campsite, a small flutter of worry swam around in his chest about their reaction when they saw him. Had they changed their mind about a tour? He was still listed on the duty roster, so the Lawrences must have still been there.

Kyle's feet felt heavy as he approached, and uncertainty filled his stomach. He felt a bit queasy, actually. But as he approached, and saw the smiling family, he sped up.

Elizabeth looked as though she hadn't just been kidnapped. Her smile was brilliant, and she looked peaceful and relaxed while holding the picnic basket. Her parents each had their art bags slung over their shoulders.

"Good morning," Kyle said. "Where would you like to go today?"

"Somewhere beautiful," Mrs. Lawrence said, "where we can see the mountains in all of their blues so that we can try to capture them with our paints."

"Let me think," Kyle said, and rubbed at his jaw. "I think I know the spot. It's a bit of a walk, though. An hour, perhaps more."

"Then we had best start," Elizabeth said.

They set off on the trail, occasionally crossing paths with another tour group. It was a beautiful day. Birds sang, the scent of the conifer trees filled their senses, and there wasn't a cloud to be seen through the tall trees above them.

Once, a doe and her late summer fawn darted out before them and then away into the woods, and the family gasped in delight before setting off again.

"Look at these tiny pinecones!" Elizabeth suddenly squealed, dropping to her heels to examine the ground.

Kyle kneeled next to her. "Those come from hemlock trees," he told her. He glanced around, and then pointed. "There's one."

"I must sketch it," Elizabeth said, setting down the picnic basket and pulling out her sketchbook. A few moments later, she put it and the pencil away, giving him a grateful smile. "I appreciate you stopping."

"Why wouldn't I?" Kyle asked, surprised. "I'm glad you enjoy nature. So do I."

"Not everyone does," Mr. Lawrence said. "I'm glad our Elizabeth has someone near her age to talk to who also enjoys it."

Kyle glanced at Elizabeth, who was flushing slightly. He reached for the picnic basket. "It's not much further. Let me carry this for you."

"Thank you," she said softly.

They started to walk again, and Kyle led them up a gently sloping path. He turned around and walked backward for a moment, grinning. "Okay, here we are. Just ahead a few paces. But careful, there are a few roots that are raised above the soil. You don't want to trip."

Eager expressions appeared on the Lawrence family's faces. As they stepped forward, to an area that was perfectly cleared away to admire the view, all of them stood, jaws open and eyes wide.

Kyle didn't blame them. He wasn't sure a single person came here and didn't feel awe at the majestic beauty before them. The mountains, in several shades of blue, rose in the distance. Mist clung to the distant trees, and above, a lone hawk glided. There was nothing more perfect, and breathtaking, and stunning than this view.

Unless he thought about Elizabeth.

"This is perfection," Mrs. Lawrence said, hastily getting out her paints.

"Mama, there looked to be a good spot just a short distance away. May Kyle and I go set out the picnic?" Elizabeth asked.

"Of course," her mother said, though the worried look that flashed in her eyes belied the ease in her voice.

"We'll stay close," Kyle promised. "Where you can see us."

Her mother nodded, and turned back to her paints. Elizabeth picked up the basket, and they walked about thirty feet away, still able to see her parents.

"Are you doing okay?" Kyle asked, wasting no time. "After what happened, I mean."

"I am," she told him. "Does it sound strange that it almost doesn't seem real? Papa says once it's all sunk in, and the shock has worn off, I may feel differently."

"Your father is a smart man," Kyle said.

"I know," Elizabeth said, smiling up at him. She reached into the basket and pulled out a small red and white checked tablecloth and shook it out, setting it onto the ground.

"What of you?" she asked, her voice low as she sank to the ground. "Your leg?"

"Fine," Kyle told her. "Just a little achy. But I'd do it all again in a heartbeat, just to find you."

"Believe it or not," Elizabeth told him, "the last few days have been some of the happiest of my life."

"Because of all of the things you've seen?" Kyle asked, though he hoped for a different answer.

A tiny smile with a hint of a tease played on her mouth. It was all he could do to look away. As soon as his eyes moved back to her eyes, she reached over, and her soft fingers brushed his.

"I want to ask you something," Elizabeth said, leaning in closely. "And you must promise to answer me truthfully."

"Of course," Kyle said quickly.

She glanced toward her parents, and his eyes followed hers. Her parents were not paying them any attention. Slowly, Elizabeth moved closer to him, and then still closer. Kyle froze, not quite knowing what to do. A breath later, her face was inches from his.

Chapter 17

Elizabeth knew she was close to Kyle. Too close. But she couldn't stop herself. Slowly, she settled back on her heels, as though she'd only been leaning forward to adjust herself. Not to kiss him. Which had been every bit her intention, until she remembered that they weren't alone and his job was at stake. And, of course, she wasn't completely sure yet how he felt about her.

"You promise?" she asked. "You'll answer truthfully?"

"I will," Kyle said, his warm eyes searching her face. His fingers moved, just the merest of distance, but drew closer to her own.

The action made her hope blossom, and she nodded. "When we go back," she told him, "I am going to miss you. I wondered if...if you'd like to write each other. See if whatever this is that we both seem to feel has the potential to grow?"

Kyle reached over and took her hand. Carefully, he asked, "What about Robbie? I've heard his name mentioned a few times, and I'm not the kind of man to push in between two people who are interested in each other."

He swallowed hard, and admitted, "And while I don't think you are the type of woman to play two men falsely, I also don't want any part of that."

The words should have hurt her. Could have, except for the fact that what she felt when talking to Kyle, and being in his presence, was so vastly different from Robbie. She also knew what he meant. She wasn't that kind of woman, and knew that wasn't who he was either. She had to explain. Set his mind at ease.

"Robbie is..." She was quiet for a moment. Once she'd connected her thoughts, she said, "He's not interested in anything more than friendship. As a matter of fact, I'm not even sure he wants friendship."

"What do you mean?" Kyle asked. Then he quickly added, "Unless that's too personal."

"It's not," she assured him. "I think that Robbie just liked having someone to be around. To make him look good. To," and she scrunched her face, "help with some of his classwork. To do errands. And," she added, blowing out a deep breath, "I kind of always knew that. But I liked having someone to do things with, even if I often felt alone while doing them. I'd tell myself that was a silly thing to feel. But I did. Empty. Hollow."

She gave a small laugh and shook her head. "Listen to me babble. None of that makes sense, does it?"

"It does," he told her, and his warm hand gently squeezed hers. "You need to be—deserve to be—around someone who wants you there and makes sure you know they do."

"That's why I want you," Elizabeth confessed. "To have a chance to know you better. Please, before you say anything, I know that's bold of me. Too bold. But, it's not the eighteen hundreds anymore. Even the early nineteen hundreds. Women are allowed to say such things now. If they mean it."

"I have an answer for you," Kyle said quietly. "But, I want a turn to ask you something first."

She nodded. "It's only fair."

"Is this...how you feel, because I rescued you? Or were those feelings there before that happened? I mean, I know you'd said—"

"Before." She needed no time to think. The word rushed out from her. "I've been falling in love with you since the moment we met." From his shoulders dropping and the tension on his face easing, she realized that had been a worry. How could she blame him?

"I've never had someone make me feel like my interests aren't strange. That I'm not strange. I like how you make me feel, how you don't mind my questions or curious nature. How you approve and encourage it. You see me. The real me. And you don't try and make me hide the parts you dislike."

"That wouldn't make you who you are, then," Kyle told her. He raised her hand to his lips, and brushed them against the back of her hand. "Yes. I want to write you. I want to see if something more could grow. Truthfully, I hope it will."

She smiled, her heart feeling light. Then, worry came over his face again, and her heart dropped into her stomach as he said, "But..."

"But?" Elizabeth whispered.

"I don't know where I'll be," he admitted with a frown. "Do you remember I told you I'd applied to that job at the university?" When she nodded, he continued, "If I don't get it, I need to find something. I'll be leaving here soon. I can write you, but I might not have a permanent address for you to send a reply to. I need to figure this out."

"We will," Elizabeth told him. "I know we will."

"I'm so glad you came here," Kyle told her. "And I'm glad I was asked to be your guide. I just wonder how your father knew about me."

Her brows twitched in confusion. "What do you mean? Papa asked for a guide. I just assumed you were assigned to us."

Kyle shook his head. "I don't quite understand myself, but I was told that your family had asked for me specifically."

"I wonder why," Elizabeth said, puzzling over the strange fact. Then she brightened. "Maybe Papa saw you when we got here. He is an excellent judge of character."

"Maybe," Kyle said, though doubt was in his tone. "I'm pretty sure Jeffs—Ranger Jeffs, he's in charge of the duty roster—said the letter came with the request to the park ahead of time."

"Isn't that odd," Elizabeth said, now frowning. Slowly, she shook her head. "I don't know." She was about to ask if he'd mind if she asked her father, when the crunching of leaves and the snapping of twigs alerted her to her parents joining them.

Elizabeth quickly set out the food from the picnic basket, and they spent the next hour talking and laughing, and plying Kyle with questions about the park.

When they returned to the campsite that night, Kyle bid them farewell, and just as Elizabeth was going to ask her father if he knew about Kyle being chosen as their guide, another ranger approached.

"Message for you, Mr. Lawrence," he said, handing over a small envelope.

"Out here? My goodness," her mother tittered. "It must be important."

Elizabeth stood next to her mother and watched as her father opened the message. His face fell. "We've got to return home in the morning," he said. "My brother is..." He stopped and caught his breath. "There's been an accident, and George might not have much time."

Elizabeth's hands flew to her mouth as her mother hugged her father. "I'll start packing at once," her mother said, turning toward the tent.

"Papa, Mama," Elizabeth asked. When they turned to her, she swallowed hard and took a deep breath. For some reason, she couldn't seem to draw in enough air. "May I please go after Kyle? To tell him? Give him our address to write? We might not get to say goodbye."

To her mortification, tears fell from her eyes. She was sure her parents wouldn't understand. Would say no, remark on how selfish she was. Her uncle might be dying, and she was only thinking of herself. Of seeing Kyle again.

But her mother nodded, and then reached inside of her artist bag and pulled out a small card, the ones that she gave to others with her contact information specially printed on them, when they inquired about her artwork. She handed it to Elizabeth, and whispered, "Go. Go find him."

"Thank you," Elizabeth gasped, taking the card, and then she turned, running in the direction Kyle had left, hoping she could find him.

Chapter 18

Kyle let out a yawn and rubbed at his eyes. He'd never tell anyone just how much his leg was aching, but it had taken more out of him to pretend he was fine and hold back the limp he wanted to do than he'd expected. He was grateful to be heading back for dinner and his bunk.

He looked forward to another few days with Elizabeth and her family. It would be nice to get to know her a little better, and know that when she left, they'd be writing to each other.

Somehow.

He still needed to figure that part out, since he didn't know where she'd be able to send him letters. Perhaps he could ask they be forwarded to him? Kyle wasn't quite sure how that worked, but he intended to find out. He also was going to seek transportation to the university there in Philadelphia. He'd stop by, inquire about any open positions, and keep his eyes alert for Elizabeth.

Mentally, Kyle went over his bank account. He didn't have a lot, but maybe he could manage a few days there, plus the transportation. Did he know anyone who lived nearby he could stay with?

"Kyle! Kyle, please wait!"

The sound of Elizabeth's voice, pitched with a hint of something akin to panic, caused Kyle to freeze and spin around.

"What's wrong?" he asked, catching her as she ran up to him, nearly breathless.

"We have to leave in the morning," she explained, her voice quivering. "Papa's brother is hurt or sick. I'm not sure which. But we must leave to go back. It sounds very serious, and this might be Papa's only chance to say goodbye."

Kyle's throat tightened. "I'm so sorry," he said, regret filling him, both for her father and for having their time cut so short.

"I wanted to make sure I saw you again, just in case," she told him, and thrust a small piece of paper at him.

Reaching instinctively, Kyle took it and glanced down.

"This is one of Mama's cards. It has our address. I know you don't know where you'll be in order to get my letters, but we will figure that out. Please, please write me. I will miss you and anxiously hold every letter I pen until I have a place to send them to. There's so much I want to tell you and talk about and..."

"I will," Kyle promised, reaching up to wipe away one of her tears with his thumb. "You can be sure of that. I'm glad you came after me. I might not have known. Do you know what time you are leaving?"

"I don't," she said, her blonde curls swaying as she shook her head. "But I'm sure it will be in the morning."

"Then I plan to stop by, and hope to have a few more moments with you," Kyle said. Reluctantly, he dropped his hand from her cheek. "How long before your parents expect you back?"

"I have to help pack," Elizabeth said, "so I can't be gone but a moment more. I also don't want to worry them."

He nodded. "I agree. They—and you—have been through too much the last few days." Kyle hesitated then, and reached for Elizabeth's hand, and took it, raising her palm to his lips. "I'm glad you found me."

"I am too," she whispered, her eyes locked on his as he slowly released her.

They stayed like that, still and quiet, lost in all of the words they both wanted to say but couldn't. The embrace they wanted to share but didn't dare to. Kyle eventually sighed. "You should go."

"I know." Elizabeth stepped backward, then said, "Kyle, please. Don't forget about me, and don't forget to write."

"I could never forget about you," Kyle said, hoping that she could hear the promise in his voice.

She gave him a smile, but it was too small, too sad, and a tightness squeezed around his heart. As Elizabeth disappeared from sight, Kyle hoped that wouldn't be the last memory he had of her.

That night, as he tried to get comfortable on the thin bunk mattress, Kyle tried to form a plan. A way to get to Pennsylvania quickly. He also worried about getting up in time to be able to say goodbye to Elizabeth and her parents. He couldn't let this glimpse of her, with those sad, beautiful eyes, be the last he saw for a while.

Or ever.

Before dawn, Kyle hurried to the campsite. It was quiet; most people weren't stirring yet. However, there was activity at the Lawrence campsite, and he was relieved he hadn't missed them.

"I was hoping to see you, my boy," Elizabeth's father said, coming out of the tent. "Have you a moment to walk and talk with me? I'm on my way to load these in the car."

"Of course, but let me help," Kyle said, reaching for one of the bags Mr. Lawrence was carrying.

They walked in silence to the car. Kyle wondered what the older man wanted to talk to him about. A sudden fear struck him, and he hoped the man wasn't about to say to stay away from his daughter.

Kyle glanced at the man, trying to discern what the expression on his face meant. Mr. Lawrence looked tired, and as though something was weighing heavily on his mind. Likely it was. Not only had his daughter been missing for two days, but now he'd also had bad news about his brother.

But was some of that weight about Kyle and Elizabeth? He should have asked first to be allowed to write her. What had he been thinking? Kyle clenched his jaw. He was stupid. Impulsive.

"Kyle," Mr. Lawrence finally said.

He looked over. "Sir?"

"How do you feel about driving back with us to Philadelphia?" Mr. Lawrence suddenly asked.

Kyle had been setting the heavy bag into the trunk of the car. Had the man asked a moment sooner, it would have likely landed on his foot, he was so shocked at the question. *I must have heard wrong,* he thought.

"Excuse me?" Kyle asked.

"I wondered if you'd consider coming back with us. To give a lecture at the university I work at. Perhaps even accept a job as my assistant."

"Your assistant?" Kyle wasn't even sure the words had escaped him. It felt as though all of his breath—and his strength—had fled. His jaw flapped in a most disorientating way, he was sure, but his thoughts were so scrambled, Kyle couldn't seem to stop himself.

"I got your letter, and wanted to see the sharp young man who'd sent it. You see, your letter was put in my office mailbox as a suggestion to become *my* assistant. I have complete permission to hire one, and I would like someone knowledgeable about nature." Mr. Lawrence studied him.

"I...I mean...is that how you knew me? But, you...I mean, are you..." Kyle shook his head, trying to align his thoughts with his words. It wasn't working.

"If you have doubts, come with us. I could use another driver to get us back home quicker. You can drive, can't you?"

"Yes, sir," Kyle said, nearly stammering.

"Good. We could just drive straight through, switching off you and I. That also gives us time to talk. Time for you to learn about the job. If you aren't interested, I'll pay your bus fare to wherever else you want to go, or I'll help you find a job somewhere in town, if you want to stay."

"Why would you do that?" Kyle asked, finally able to form a coherent sentence.

Mr. Lawrence shrugged, and grew a thoughtful look on his face. "Instinct tells me to, my boy. I just have a way of knowing about things, and the moment I held your letter...I knew you were right. Right for the school, right for me, right for...Elizabeth."

Elizabeth. Kyle's heart pounded. "Does that mean you approve of our writing?" he ventured. "I ought to have asked first before promising her I would."

"I'd hope you'd do more than just write if you lived in the same town," Mr. Lawrence boomed in laughter. "You'll have my blessing, and perhaps...one day my daughter's hand if she agrees."

Kyle couldn't stop the grin that came over his face. "I would like that, sir." He frowned then. "But I have to get permission. After all, I am employed here for another week."

"Already done, my boy," Mr. Lawrence said. "I hope you don't mind. All you need to do is pack. And," the man said, holding up a hand, "I promise to stop interfering in your life and your job after that. But I knew you didn't have much time left here, and after what happened to our family, I was hoping it would be allowed."

Kyle's eyebrows raised. "You're friends with someone mighty influential," he guessed.

"Went to school with and tutored a few of the rascals," Mr. Lawrence chuckled. "I called in a few favors, yes. But the choice is yours. You don't have to say yes. I will understand if you want to find your own way there. I shouldn't have interfered."

"I'll meet you here in an hour," Kyle promised, then wasted no time, jogging back to pack and tell the other rangers goodbye.

Everything had happened so fast, he wasn't sure he could quite believe it.

He also couldn't wait to see Elizabeth's face when she found out.

Chapter 19

"Do you have everything?" Elizabeth's mother asked, taking a last glance around. "You won't want to leave anything behind."

I already am. Kyle is here, Elizabeth thought, though she didn't speak, and just nodded.

"I'm sorry we have to leave sooner than expected," her mother said, as they started toward where her father was loading the last of their bags into the car.

"It can't be helped," Elizabeth said. "Besides, we need to check on Uncle George. Just...just in case."

"Yes," her mother said quietly. "I only hope it's not serious."

A moment later, they rounded a gentle curve on the walkway, and Elizabeth spotted the car. Her father stood beside it, and then her heart leaped. Kyle was standing there as well, talking to her father. She'd have a chance to tell him goodbye!

"Go on." Her mother smiled.

Unable to stop the skip in her step, Elizabeth hurried over, and beamed up at Kyle. "You're here! I'm so glad. I didn't think I'd get to see you again." She stood a proper distance away, though her hands twitched with longing to touch him.

"You'll be seeing a lot of me over the next few days," Kyle said, almost shyly, as he ran a hand through his hair. "I hope that's all right."

"What do you mean?" Elizabeth asked. Then her eyes widened. "You're not in your uniform. Where is it?" At a chuckle, she glanced at her parents, who were smiling broadly.

"Your father has asked me to drive back with you to Philadelphia," Kyle said.

"He has?" Elizabeth gasped, clapping her hands together in surprise.

"Yes, that way I can drive part of the time to get you there faster. And he's..." Kyle shook his head. "It's still not sunk in. He's asked me if I want to be his assistant."

Elizabeth stood for a moment in shock, then let out a most undignified shriek and flung herself at Kyle, then pulled away to do the same to her father, wrapping her arms around his neck. "Papa!" she cried out happily.

Her father laughed as he hugged her tightly. "I couldn't have my daughter be sad. Perhaps a little more time between the two of you will let you see if something blossoms, before you see that other young man, who is not at all the right kind of person for you."

"I hope so," Elizabeth said, squeezing him tightly. "Oh, Papa, did you arrange all of this? Everything?"

He laughed, but didn't answer. "Time to go, I think. Everyone climb in. Kyle, this first leg, come sit with me, my boy. Let's talk about the university."

Elizabeth slid into the backseat, and her mother sat next to her. "Mama," she said quietly, leaning over slightly, "I don't know what to say."

"Hopefully it's 'goodbye' to Robbie," her mother teased. "I never liked him."

Elizabeth laughed. Her heart was so full, there was no room for words. Life so rarely had moments like these, where all of the hopes a person had came true. She was going to accept, enjoy, and be thankful for every second of this trip. While she didn't know the future, no one did, she would hope that things continued to work favorably because at this moment, she couldn't imagine not being with Kyle.

The trip passed quickly, far too much so for her liking. Each time they stopped and switched drivers, Elizabeth couldn't stop grinning. As they got just a few hours away, her parents sat in the front, and Kyle, planning to accept the position as her father's assistant, sat next to her, holding her hand.

Elizabeth took pleasure in pointing out things to Kyle, taking her turn to play tour guide, much as he'd done for her. She pointed out landmarks such as her favorite café, the library, several parks, and the place she bought her sketchbooks and pencils.

As they drove past the university, Kyle stared at it in wonder. "I can't believe how large it is," he said, taking in the large buildings with decorative arched windows. "Look at that stunning brick and stonework."

"It's beautiful, isn't it?" Elizabeth asked. "I love being on the grounds."

"It's the third most beautiful thing I've ever seen," Kyle said.

"What are the first two?" Elizabeth asked curiously.

Kyle smiled at her. "You, of course, and then Shenandoah National Park."

Chapter 20

Over the next year, there wasn't much of the city that Kyle didn't explore with Elizabeth or her family. Hours were spent together in museums, gardens, and little restaurants just talking. He had dinner several times a week with her family as well, even getting to meet her uncle, who was now fully recovered from his unfortunate accident involving an escaped snake from his classroom.

It seemed that a love of nature in all forms filled her family. Kyle was glad to be sharing in that, and learning more than he'd ever imagined possible. Elizabeth's father was a brilliant man, and he felt proud to be his assistant.

"Are you ready?" Elizabeth asked, coming into Mr. Lawrence's classroom.

"I am," Kyle said, snapping his bag closed. "Only two dozen papers to grade tonight."

She laughed. "Well then, I promise not to keep you out too late." She reached for his arm, and they strolled out of the school. Elizabeth paused at the top of a flight of steps and frowned. "That's Robbie," she told him, pointing out the man he'd been curious to see. It had surprised him that he hadn't yet.

Tall and lanky, with overly oiled hair, Robbie stood, talking to a young woman. As they got closer, they could hear the conversation.

"Megan, you only got me a C on this paper. Now I might fail the class." Robbie shook the paper at her.

"That sounds familiar," Elizabeth said, with a small shake of her head. "And I don't miss it. What a fool I was."

"Not at all," Kyle assured her.

"That's what I like about you," Elizabeth said, as they stepped out into the late summer day. "You're always so kind."

"Kind," he agreed, "truthful, and enamored, among other things."

"As long as it's enamored with me," she teased.

"Only you," Kyle told her. Then, he led her to a bench. "Can we stop here a moment? I wanted to give you something."

"What is it?" Elizabeth asked curiously.

Kyle slung his bag on the bench and dug through it. When his fingers wrapped around the small box, he took a deep breath and pulled it out. "I found this the other day," he told Elizabeth, hiding it in his hand.

"Stop teasing me and show it!" she said.

Kyle opened the small velvet box, and held it toward her. Inside, the silver band held three blue sapphires, each a different shade.

"They look like the Shenandoah National Park mountains," Elizabeth gasped, unable to tear her eyes from the ring.

"I know it's not really traditional," Kyle said, suddenly nervous. "Usually, when you are asking someone to marry you, you offer a diamond. But, this felt right. I know diamonds are forever, but so are mountains. And, well…"

"You don't have to say another thing," Elizabeth told him, finally looking away from the ring and into his eyes. "Are you asking me to marry you?"

His lips twitched into a smile. "I thought you said I didn't have to say anything else."

"You don't," she agreed. "But I think you ought to, if you want the answer to be yes."

Kyle dropped onto his knee, and asked, "Elizabeth Lawrence, would you marry me and let me love you and call you my own forever?"

To his surprise, Elizabeth got down on her knees, and met him eye to eye. "Yes, Kyle," she whispered. "And I will love you and forever call you my own."

Kyle pulled the ring from the box and put it on Elizabeth's finger. A late ray from the sun made it sparkle, illuminating each of the hues of blue.

"Every time I look at this, I'm going to remember how and where we met," Elizabeth told him. "You couldn't have found a more perfect ring."

"I also couldn't have found a more perfect woman," Kyle said, standing and helping her to rise. "I will love you, Elizabeth, for longer than those mountains are blue."

When Elizabeth answered, Kyle couldn't hear it for the thudding of his heart and the rushing of joy in his ears. But as they walked to his car to go show her parents, he knew one thing. And that was he would forever be grateful he'd written that letter to the university all those months ago, and that it had found its way into the hands of the man who would bring Kyle and his daughter together.

Epilogue

Twenty years later

"Are you sure you'll be fine?" Elizabeth fretted, glancing around as her twin nineteen-year-olds pulled their suitcases from the car.

"Mama," Frank said, "don't worry. If we forget something, you can mail it."

"You assume she would," Fern said. "When in all actuality, she'd drive it up to us. Maybe even stay here and never leave."

"I would," Elizabeth agreed. She stood there, looking at her children with teary eyes. "How has the time passed so quickly? Look at you both, following in your father's footsteps."

"You two ready?" Kyle asked, coming out of the ranger station. "I'd like you to meet Jeffs. We worked together when I was a park ranger here. He's going to look after you both."

As greetings were exchanged, Elizabeth smiled sadly, already missing her children. When they'd both said they wanted to join the summer program to train as park guides, she'd been excited at first. And then quite nervous.

Now, watching them leave, following behind Ranger Jeffs without even looking back, she wasn't quite sure how she felt.

"It's strange," Kyle said, watching them. "We weren't much older when we met. Who knows? One of them—or both—might come back with a sweetheart."

Elizabeth's eyes widened. "I hadn't thought of that."

"Look at that," Kyle said, pointing in the distance. "Remember that spot?"

"I do," she agreed, and they wandered over to the place they'd met, so many years ago.

Elizabeth looked down at the ring she wore, and then held her hand up. "Look how perfectly it matches," she told him. "I'll never tire of looking at it."

"I'll never tire of looking at you," Kyle said, and wrapped an arm around her.

The two stood, watching as couples and families and park rangers darted around the national park. Though the years had brought many changes, in so many ways things were just the same.

As the two left the park, the twisty roads and spectacular views before them, Elizabeth tipped her head back to the sky. A few birds traveled lazily above, and then vanished as the car tipped low and the trees filled the sky. She remembered all that time ago when she'd first arrived, seeing these same trees as her father drove this exact road, and then the moment when the handsome park ranger had introduced himself.

The words Kyle had said to her when he proposed marriage to her sprang to mind, and she repeated them, only changing them slightly. "I will love you, Kyle, for longer than those mountains are blue."

And when he answered with his own I love you, his voice completed the peaceful feeling within her, as the warm breeze rushed across her face from the open car window. The sweet sounds of birds filled her ears, and off in the distance, the mountains so tall and impressive looked down on them, promising to be there forever and always, for whoever might want to visit them.

The Complicated History of Shenandoah National Park

When asked if I wanted to join this multi-author series and write about a national park, I said yes. Living right by one of the Shenandoah National Park entrances, and being a lover of history, this particular national park has always held a fascination, and a bit of sorrow, for me as the years go by and more is revealed about the families who inhabited the land before it was established as a national park in 1936.

I wanted to put this note in because I want to make sure that any reader who is aware of Shenandoah National Park's complex history in forcing out thousands of people who called the land home understands that while I don't talk about that much in my story, I am not minimizing in any way whatsoever the terrible and maybe even underhand way in which the land was taken from those who had lived there happily and peacefully.

While there were many who left willingly, with the hopes for a better future elsewhere after selling their land to the government, there are many, many stories of those who were evicted through eminent domain and did not want to leave the place they called home.

This book is written with the intention of being a piece of fiction, where the story takes place within Shenandoah National Park, and talks a little of its creation, its beauty, the species, and the lore of the park, and done so through *the lens of that time*. Unlike now, where we have an absolute wealth of information at our fingertips just a few clicks away, that wasn't the case in the early 1900s. The average person had no idea the tourist attraction being built was at the expense of others. It wasn't until time went on that the extent of what was done to create this national park was known.

While the home and landowners were offered a per-acre price to leave the acreage that was occupied (3,000 land tracts, originally 160,000 acres, though later the park expanded to around 200,000 acres), and some did, others pleaded to stay. A few of the homeowners were able to remain until death, but with a good number of rules applied to them. Those who didn't own land but lived there (as in tenants who may have cared for the land and any buildings for the owners who did not live there) faced a different set of complications. This book takes place before the final removal of those families, beginning at the park's opening.

At the time of the Shenandoah National Park opening, not all of the trails or overlooks were ready, nor the facilities that would be slowly added on. Only a portion of the land was available for those early tourists, as Skyline Drive was not completed yet and would not be until 1939. Skyline Drive is a 105-mile scenic byway and the only public road that runs through the national park. Today, it meets with the Blue Ridge Parkway, another scenic road.

On Skyline Drive are many scenic overlooks, and the road runs right along the crest of the Blue Ridge Mountains. There are four ways to access it, all in Virginia. Front Royal, Thornton Gap, Swift Run Gap, and Rockfish Gap.

As true for many of the federally designated parks, wildernesses, and monuments, the Shenandoah National Park's landscape, even today, reflects centuries of human activity that predates its status as a national park. If you look closely, you may still see fragments of the past, such as shards of glass or old tools, and you will walk past trees and rocks that were there at the park's opening and long before.

Although a few visual reminders of the people who lived, worked, and played there remain within Shenandoah National Park, those represent only a fraction of the homes and churches, mills, orchards, schools, and other buildings scattered throughout that existed long before the park was imagined and then established. If you wander through the forest, human-built piles of rocks turned into walls to mark property boundaries still exist, and indicate where farmsteads and homesteads used to be.

The majority of the pre-park buildings, even the orchards and gardens, were intentionally destroyed or left to decay in the years leading up to and following the park's establishment. It's hard to imagine, or perhaps even know, how many buildings were destroyed.

While today, there is much more information dedicated to the history of this park, including around three hundred letters written by the original inhabitants of Shenandoah National Park when they asked to stay in their homes, many tourists who do not stop into these visitor stations or read up on the park are unaware of the fact that so many people lost their generational homes and lands so the park could be built.

If you ever go to Shenandoah National Park yourself, consider taking a moment to enjoy and be grateful such pristine beauty was preserved so that generations could experience the wooded areas and natural wonders of our planet, but also remember that everything in life for another to enjoy comes at a cost, even if we may not know it at the time.

For more research, both past and present, and to see photographs of Shenandoah National Park, you can visit this website:

https://www.nps.gov/shen/learn/historyculture/index.htm

Note from Author

Thank you for taking the time to read *Elizabeth Shenandoah Bride.*

Could I ask for one small favor? Reviews like yours on Amazon mean so much to me and help others to find my books! Even just a single line means a lot!

Also...

Want a FREE book?

Stop by my website to get your no strings attached **FREE book**. It's my gift to you, as a thank you for reading this one.

www.sarahlambbooks.com

Keep reading...

You can find all of the National Park Bride books right
here!
https://www.amazon.com/dp/B0F9VRGMWP
And you can also find all of Sarah's books here:
https://www.amazon.com/stores/Sarah-Lamb/author/B
098H3SGLK

About the Author

Sarah writes captivating characters and clean romance that's anything BUT boring! From heartbreaking moments to heartwarming tales, get swept away in either historical or small town romance that pulls you in until the last page.

Nestled in the Blue Ridge Mountains of Virginia where she's married to her Texan husband, you'll find Sarah creating her next book, homeschooling her two boys, or volunteering in her community.

Want more of Sarah's books? Find them all on Amazon!

https://www.amazon.com/stores/Sarah-Lamb/author/B098H3SGLK